CW01498472

Naughty Bits (Revised)

By Selena Kitt

eXcessica publishing

Naughty Bits (Revised) © 2011 by Selena Kitt

Excessica LLC
P.O. Box 127
Alpena, MI 49707

To order additional copies of this book, contact:
books@excessicapublishing.com
www.excessica.com

Cover art © 2011 Michael Mantas
Third Edition "Naughty Bits, Revised"—June 2011
Second Edition "Foreign Exchange"—December 2010
First Edition "Naughty Bits"— May 2008

AUTHORS'S NOTE

I have a bit of a story to tell you about this story.

Once upon a time back in 2008, this book was published under the title "Naughty Bits" without that annoying "Revised" afterward. It was a taboo story involving sibling incest. That book sat happily on Amazon's virtual shelves for two years.

But that is not the book you have right now on your e-reader or in your hands. Instead, this book is the "revised" version. In "Naughty Bits (Revised)", the brother and sister are not biologically related (they are step-relations), so there is no actual biological incest that ever takes place.

Why the change?

That's a long story, and you can skip it if you like, but if you are an erotica reader who enjoys reading adult *fantasies* (and I emphasize that word *fantasy*) about taboo topics, this tale might be of some interest to you and may even affect your future reading choices.

On December 9, 2010, I was contacted by CreateSpace (Amazon's Print on Demand service) who publishes my print books. They informed me that several of my titles had been removed for violating their "content guidelines." When I consulted their guidelines I found them so vague as to be useless—were they saying my content was illegal? Public domain? Stolen? Offensive? (All of these were on the list). When I inquired as to the specifics of the violation, they were not forthcoming, and sent a form letter response stating that Amazon "may, in its sole discretion, at any time, refuse to list or distribute any content that it deems inappropriate."

On Sunday, December 12, 2010 the print titles that had been removed had now disappeared from the Kindle store. I have over fifty titles selling on Amazon, all of them in erotic fiction categories. The only thing these three singled-out titles had in common, besides being written by me? They were all erotic incest fantasy fiction.

About this time, I heard that two other authors both had erotic incest-related titles removed from Amazon's site.

After some research, I discovered more authors whose books had also been removed. As the night wore on, and public outcry about censorship and banned books began on Twitter at #amazonfail and #amazoncensors and on their own Kindle Boards, more and more incest-related erotica titles began to disappear from the Amazon site, so that the "Kindle Incest" search page began to look like Swiss cheese.

I'm quite sure, although I can't prove it, that all of this was a result of the controversy about the self-published book The Pedophile's Guide to Love and Pleasure by Phillip R. Greaves (that link is no longer active on Amazon, by the way). It went on sale, according to Amazon's book page, on October 28, 2010. On November 10, 2010, the link disappeared. Before Amazon pulled the book, they issued this statement:

"Amazon believes it is censorship not to sell certain books simply because we or others believe their message is objectionable. Amazon does not support or promote hatred or criminal acts, however, we do support the right of every individual to make their own purchasing decisions."

And when the L.A. Times did an interview with Russ Grandinetti, the "head of content for Amazon.com's Kindle business," he reiterated Amazon's mission statement: *"Our vision is [to make] every book ever written, in any language, in print or out of print, all available within 60 seconds."*

So much for those noble ideas and goals. They removed Mr. Greaves' book and then, a month later, started removing other erotic titles from their site. Three of mine were victims.

I want to be clear that while the subject of incest fantasy may not appeal to some, there is no underage contact in any of my work, and I make that either explicitly clear in all my stories or I state it up front in the book's disclaimer. I don't condone or support actual incest, just as someone who writes mysteries about serial killers wouldn't condone killing. What I write is fiction. It's fantasy, not reality.

Certainly what I write is controversial, but it seems as undeserving of censorship as... well...

As fellow author, Will Belegon, noted, if Amazon is going to start pulling books with incest in them: "I just re-read Genesis 19: 30-38 and realized that Lot's daughters got him drunk, had sex with him and bore sons. I demand you follow your clear precedent and remove The Bible from Kindle."

Or perhaps Amazon should create a new television ad to follow their "clear precedent" and ban the book the woman is reading in an advertisement on her Kindle ("Sleepwalking" by Amy Bloom) which tells the story of a nineteen-year-old boy who has a sexual encounter with his stepmother, which, in some states, is legally incest. Oh, but wait, Amazon says incest between step-relations is ok. There's logic for you.

If Amazon had clear guidelines that were applied to all publishers across every platform and enforced consistently, this would be a moot issue. By not clearly stating their position and choosing books either arbitrarily or based on searches of top-rated titles which are the most visible titles in the genre, they seem to be deliberately hiding a clear case of discrimination and what amounts to censorship (albeit ipso facto and not by a government body but rather a retailer) because of their lack of transparency.

I have said before and I'll say it again—I have no problem with a company deciding what they will and will not sell, but I do have a problem with the way Amazon has handled this. They could have come to the publishers and told them about their new guidelines, given them time to prepare their authors and make other arrangements. Anthologies that contained offending material, for example, could have been reworked and re-uploaded instead of being removed, without any penalty in loss in ranking.

Instead, they clandestinely removed titles, informed authors and publishers days or weeks later, and most importantly, refused to tell anyone what they were doing or why. They should, in my opinion, be clear about what is and isn't acceptable. This "ban as we go" way of doing things is just going to move from one hot button topic to the next. If you're a business, and you're going to make a policy, *then make one.* Readers and authors have a right to know where Amazon stands. That's just good business.

Because of Amazon's actions, I have personally self-censored my books, releasing a new version of *Under Mr. Nolan's Bed* without the father/daughter incest angle at all titled, *Plaid Skirt Confessions,* and a different version of *Naughty Bits* without the sibling incest titled, *Foreign Exchange.* I've clearly stated in the descriptions that they are reworked versions of the originals, so readers will know.

I've also now released a special Amazon edition of all of the banned books as well, allowing Amazon customers access to the stories with the taboo aspects included but without the offending biological incest. Amazon, apparently, has decided that as long as the incest takes place between consenting step-relations, it's okay in their book. Until that changes (and who knows when and how that might happen—Amazon sure isn't going to tell us!) you, Dear Reader, will have access on Amazon to my taboo collection, albeit in a somewhat altered form.

In speculating on the motivations of Amazon's actions, as they have not been forthcoming with any statement or explanation, I am sure they responded out of reactionary fear. While I am not a lawyer, constitutional scholar or legal expert on free speech and intellectual freedom, I am an author and publisher and know that, regardless of the technical legalities of Amazon's actions, buckling to this pressure and the removal of books is hurting their bottom line. It's damaging relationships with readers, authors, and publishers as well as organizations such as the American Library Association and the ACLU, among others, who are interested in supporting free speech. I should also note that I am a professional psychologist and, while no longer licensed (by personal choice) or working in the field, it's clear that when individuals and organizations fail to recognize the difference between fantasy and reality, problems such as this result.

If any of this concerns you as a reader of erotica, please continue to support intellectual freedom and free speech. Let Amazon and other retailers know your preferences. Inform the media when you discover incidents of this type of retail censorship.

The truth is, you are in a majority and you are very important to retailers. According to the numbers being thrown around, Amazon is alienating its ebook "power-buyer" audience by banning erotic fiction. Those protesting about erotic fiction on retail shelves are actually just a vocal minority. The reality is that you, the "power-buyers," are the majority.

And if you don't speak up, who will? Do you really want your choices being limited by a vocal minority? Please don't be a part of the silent majority. Make a difference. Let yourself be heard. Be a vocal consumer. There's nothing wrong with your choice of reading material. We all know the saying, "Guns don't kill people—people kill people," right? The same is true for fiction. *Fantasy doesn't hurt anyone.* Only people can do that. Reading erotica isn't wrong. It's simply a preference—and a perfectly valid one.

Let freedom ring!

Thank you for your support.

XOXO

Selena

Chapter One

If my mum and dad found out about my collection of porn in the shed, I knew they'd both kick-off and I'd be sleeping under a bench in the Underground, buying papers to keep me warm—instead of buying them like I was now, looking for a job. As it was, they were on at me to find something, and fast. I didn't get why I had to figure it all out, what I wanted to do with the rest of my life. What was the rush?

My stepsister, Dawn, got to preen around the health club at her summer job. So why was I supposed to find something "responsible?" Dawn had been living at home since she finished school, aside from a couple of disastrous attempts at living with a roommate that my parents had ended up paying more for in the long run, anyway.

My parents made all sorts of exceptions for her. They thought she'd had it rough, since her own mum had died when she was so little. Never mind that my own dad had taken off on my mum when I was a baby and I'd never seen the bloke—we guys were supposed to suck it up or something. And really my mum was like her mum, even though she really wasn't, and her dad was like my dad, even though he really wasn't, and we were just like brother and sister, grown up together since we were tots.

But somehow Dawn still got all the special treatment. Maybe it was just because she was a girl. I had hoped that her laziness, or as my mother put it, her "lack of focus," might pave the way for me to spend some time loafing off after I finished school, too, but no—apparently, Dawn got the welcome mat, but I got threatened with the boot. I didn't get it.

I shut the back door and looked up at the sky. We didn't get days like this in Surrey very often—so bright and blue and clear. We spent most of our time walking around in the usual London grey, looking at a hazy kind of film over the sun. Days like today made me remember being a kid, endless summers with no responsibilities, no cares, no worries. So much for that, I thought, flopping the paper down on the patio table and glaring at it.

I sat in one of the folding chairs and took a highlighter out of my pocket. The first thing I circled was a construction company. Maybe I could find something working outside— get a tan, build some muscle. That might lead to getting a girlfriend, I thought hopefully. That got me to thinking about Julie Entwistle, the girl rumoured to wear nothing under her skirts in sixth form. She sat right next to me in English, but I never did see anything—not that I didn't try. For a girl who was supposed to be a slag, she sure kept her legs together a lot.

Thinking about Julie's skirt, and more importantly, what might be found under her skirt, made my jeans uncomfortably tight. I shifted in the chair, shoving at my crotch and turning the page of the newspaper, re-focusing my efforts. The ad that caught my eye read: Exotic dancers wanted to perform at private, solo, and bachelor parties... I snorted—so much for trying to focus. Now my cock was officially hard. I glanced over at the shed, thinking of the boards my dad stored in there that "might come in handy" some day. They came in handy for hiding my porn collection.

I folded the paper up and tucked it under my arm, heading toward the shed. My dad's toolbox doubled as a step stool and was perfect for sitting on. I dug under the boards, pulling out my meagre collection. Two *Playboys* and a *Penthouse,* although the latter was a "Letters" edition, and the stories were pretty hot. The last one was my favourite, a magazine called *Naughty Bits,* which was way more hardcore than the others. I'd never seen another one before or since, although believe me, I'd looked.

I opened it up to my favourite page, and there she was. Blonde, although clearly dyed because her pubes were dark, a full-breasted and full-bodied girl—really unusual for most spreads nowadays where the models were like stick figures. This woman was, well... a woman.

The next best part was the layout itself—a girl all alone on her bed looking at porn. Did girls do that? I loved how she rolled over and spread her legs, revealing that there was nothing under her skirt. She started masturbating, and would you look at that, next page, here comes her brother. Probably it was her boyfriend, but I had this fantasy in my head that it was her brother. And the next thing you know, she's sucking him off. God, how I wished it was that easy. *Hi there, whoops, didn't mean to interrupt, but since I'm here, zzziiiip, flop, here's this hard cock you can suck...*

I unzipped my jeans and tugged them down a little, slipping my hand into my boxers. Nowhere near as big as the guy positioning his cock at her pink little hole (I loved that picture, her fingers spreading herself open for him like that. Gah! Did girls do that?) but respectable enough—nice and thick, and most definitely stiff. She did it for me, every time. I started masturbating, my eyes skipping from the wet pink of her cunt to her thick, dark pink nipples. I spent some time there, wanking away and staring at the slit between her legs. She spread it open with both hands, and there was a little hole there, right where I wanted to slide my cock, a small dark hollow leading to heaven.

I got myself good and worked up before starting to turn the next page, because it was my favourite, and it was the image I always came to—her arse up in the air, his cum sliding down her arsehole and cunt. I was looking forward to that image, still staring between her legs. I only stopped for a moment, breathless, to turn the page, and I saw something that made my cock jump and my heart race. There was writing in the margin, near the page number. An arrow toward the girl (God, look how that thick cum slid down that pink slit!) and the words, "She looks like me."

That was Dawn's handwriting—the fat, curly letters, the heart over the "i." My stepsister had been looking at my porn? Why, I wondered? If she wanted to get me in trouble, she could have taken it to my mum. Instead, she just wrote in the margins. And what she'd written! I flushed. I knew the girl looked remarkably like my stepsister—the dyed blonde hair, the full body, the mischievous eyes, the slanted smile—that was Dawn. Was she just making an observation? Was she implying that I lusted after her?

I didn't have any more time to think about it. Someone was knocking on the shed door! I stood, tucking my cock back in and zipping up, shoving the magazines back under the pile of boards.

"David!" It was Dawn. Of course, who else? My parents wouldn't be home for hours—it was only ten in the morning.

"What?" I called, trying to sound impatient. I tucked my paper back under my arm, grabbed a can of insect spray off the shelf and opened the door.

She was standing there in a white bikini, the flesh of her breasts spilling over the top. My cock, with barely enough chance to wane as it was, jumped to life again at the sight.

"Jesus, Dawn!" I made a face. "Put some clothes on."

"It's gonna be sunny and warm all day." She put her hands on her hips and drew my eyes there. "I'm spending my time catching rays!"

"Whatever." I stepped out of the shed into the fresh air.

"What were you doing in there?" She smirked, peering into the dim shed.

I waved the insect repellant at her. "Big-arse spider out on the patio table."

"Sure there was." She moved toward the lounge chair where she had spread a towel. How long had she been out here, I wondered?

I put the can on the table. "There was. It's obviously crawled off somewhere. Maybe it's on your lounge chair."

She stuck her tongue out at me. "Quit being such a pain in the arse. I'm in a good mood and you're not going to spoil it."

Dawn positioned her chair, looking up toward the sun as she did, and then crawled on. Her bikini bottoms rode up between her cheeks and I flashed on the picture in *Naughty Bits* that I'd found the writing on—her arse up in the air, cum sliding down her slit. I sat down at the table, putting the paper in my lap to cover my erection.

"What's got you so perky?" I scowled.

She was lying on her back, now, and she lifted her sunglasses to look at me. "It's my first day on holiday, you git! Two whole weeks off work!"

I turned my chair away from her, opening my paper back up. My cock was still throbbing and watching her oil herself up out of the corner of my eye wasn't helping. She was slathering lotion all over, rubbing it into the creases, even between her toes. I could smell the stuff, like coconuts, as if a tropical smell was supposed to make you turn darker.

"You find anything in there yet?" She dropped the lotion next to her chair and leaned back. Her breasts jiggled in the white bikini top when she did, and I couldn't help watching. Seeing real flesh move was different from looking at a picture in a magazine. I found myself wondering what it would feel like to touch her there, just the top of her breast, all shiny from the oil. I flushed.

"No." I turned my eyes back to the paper. "There's nothing out there."

"Well, mum and dad won't let you scrounge off them forever, you know." She threw an arm up over her head.

"Sod off!" I rolled my eyes. "I'm not the one who's still living with my parents at twenty-five."

I stood up, deciding to go into the house. Maybe take another shower. I felt hot and sweaty, although it wasn't really that warm out here, yet.

"Hey." Dawn lifted her sunglasses again. Her eyes were soft, and so was her smile. "You wanna do something for me?"

"If it involves lotion and your back, forget it." I reached for the back door. "I'm your brother, remember?"

She stuck her tongue out. "If you're going in the house... maybe you could bring out one of dad's bottles of wine?"

I raised my eyebrows at her. "The good stuff?"

"Yeah." She grinned. "Why not? Let's celebrate my holiday. You're eighteen now."

I opened the door, heading into the house. The kitchen was to the right, and I threw the paper on the table, squatting down in front of the wine rack. I found a bottle of dad's favourite wine. It was almost full, but had been uncorked. I grabbed it, turning back to the door. Dawn was adjusting her straps when I looked out, lifting her breasts as she did. I sighed, going out.

"Here." I put the bottle next to her chair.

"Ta," she smiled. I turned to go and she grabbed my arm, lowering her voice. "Come on, David. Don't be mean. Stay and keep me company. Pull up a chair and soak up some sun."

I pulled a lounge chair over next to hers and adjusted it. From this vantage point, I didn't have to worry about her seeing where my eyes were going—and they were running—up and down the lengths of her legs, over her full hips and soft belly, toward the rise of her breasts. They lingered there, watching her breathe, and my cock felt like it was going to burst. I was going to have to take a very long shower.

She picked up the bottle, uncorking it. "No glasses?" She turned to smile at me.

I shrugged. "You want me to go get some?"

"I don't have the lurgy." She took a swig and held the bottle out to me. "Here."

I grabbed the bottle and took a taste, making a face. I wasn't much of a drinker—the stuff tasted awful. I handed it back to her.

"Aren't you hot?" she asked. "Why don't you strip down to your pants?"

I flushed. If I stripped, she might see my erection. She slid her sunglasses down her nose, raising her eyebrows.

"Come on, it's nothing I haven't seen before, you know."

I shrugged, unbuttoning my shirt and tossing it over on the table. I stood to undo my jeans, and I saw Dawn's eyes move to my crotch as she took another swig of wine. She handed it to me, and I took a long swallow, my eyes burning. I took my time, willing my cock into submission. It partially worked. I pushed my jeans down my hips, stepping out of them and laying back on the lounger wearing just my boxers

She handed me the wine again, and I drank some more, starting to feel the effects already. My head felt lighter.

"So do you have any interviews?" She took another drink from the wine bottle and passed it.

"I had one." I took a swig. I was getting used to the taste. "But it was some insurance thing. It was all a bit dodgy."

"Nothing else?"

"Can we change the subject?" I glowered at the wine bottle as I held it up to my lips. It glittered in the sun. "I'm tired of talking about 'my future.'"

She cocked her head at me, frowning. "Poor little bit." She sighed. "Being grown-up sucks."

"Wish someone would have told me." I shaded my eyes against the sun. It was really bright. "I thought it was gonna be crackin', you know, getting to do whatever you want..."

She laughed. "I wish." She handed me the bottle again. "I know you'll find something. You just have to keep at it."

I snorted. "You sound just like mum. 'You need to try harder, David.'"

"Let's change the subject," she agreed. "Let's talk about sex."

I choked on the wine going down my throat, some of it dribbling onto my chin. "Not the conversation I need to be having with my sister. Let's talk about me finding a bloody job, all right?"

"Have you ever fucked a girl?" She took the bottle back. "Come on, David, you can tell me."

I flushed, staring directly at the sun and then closing my eyes, seeing a bright spot where it had been. "No."

"I didn't think so." She nudged my arm with the bottle.

"Is it that obvious?" I took a swallow, handing it back with my eyes still closed.

Her voice was soft as she said, "No wonder you toss-off so much in the shed."

My eyes flew open, my jaw dropped. My face burned and I couldn't say anything.

Dawn was holding the bottle up. "Crikey! This is almost gone!"

"How long have you known?" I swallowed hard.

"Long enough." She smiled

"Are you gonna tell mum and dad?"

She was grinning now. "Oh, I don't know, that depends."

"On what?" I sat up and turned toward her.

"You know mum will throw a wobbly if she finds out you've got porn."

"Why do you think it's hidden in the shed?" I sighed miserably. "Are you going to tell?"

"I was just teasing." She sat up in her chair and faced me. "What are we, ten? I'm not a grass. So you look at porn. What bloke doesn't, right?"

I sighed, relieved. I looked at her, remembering the words written in the margins. "Say, Dawn... did you... were you looking at it?"

She grinned. "She looks an awful lot like me, doesn't she?"

I nodded, meeting her eyes. "She's my favourite."

She stood, grabbing onto the back of the chair for a moment. She started toward the house. When she got to the door, she looked back at me. "Come on."

I followed her after a moment, finding her standing in the kitchen, leaning against the table. Her bikini top was on the table, too, and I was staring at her breasts. I couldn't move, I couldn't think, I couldn't even breathe.

"You like what you see?" She cupped them and pulled on her nipples. My face was burning, but my cock was stiffening in response. "They look a lot like hers, don't they?"

I nodded in agreement. Blimey, almost exactly like the girl in *Naughty Bits!* The same little areolas, the dark pinkish nipples. My cock jumped as I watched her rub her hands over them.

"Dawn, what are you doing?" I heard the hoarseness in my own voice.

"Well, I'm a bit pissed," she admitted. "And I'm really randy, especially after watching you wanking in the shed."

"Oh, God," I groaned, putting my hand to my forehead. She was moving toward me, and my eyes fell from her breasts down to her bikini bottoms. Now that I'd seen the top, I wanted to see the rest.

"You wanna suck these?" she purred, pulling on her nipples. "Do you wanna shove your cock in my cunt, baby brother?"

I had backed up to the wall and she was leaning in toward me, not touching me, but close. She slid her hand down into her bikini, and I could see the top edge of her pubic hair.

"You wanna fuck me?" Her hand moved between her legs.

I groaned, closing my eyes against it. "Dawnie," I pleaded. "Please. Stop."

"You want to," she whispered, and I jumped when she squeezed my crotch. My cock throbbed against her hand through my boxers. "You've been wanking in the shed and looking at that girl who looks just like me and wishing it was really me all along, haven't you?"

She moved her hand between my legs, rubbing it up and down the length of my shaft through the thin material.

I groaned, "Yes. Oh God, Dawn, yes." I grabbed her hand, pushing it away. "You gotta stop. We really can't do this."

She pouted, her brow knitting. "Why not?"

"Because," I choked. "Because you're my sister."

She sighed, moving back and sliding up to sit on the table. She smiled, then, her eyes getting that mischievous glint they used to whenever we were gonna do something we'd get in big trouble for. "Well... what if we don't touch each other?"

I frowned. "What do you mean?"

She bit her lip, leaning back on the table so she was lying down. I gasped at the sight of her, spread out on the table topless, the bikini bottoms showing the clear outline of her cunt, swollen and thick. God, I wanted to see. My cock was tenting my boxers, and there wasn't a damned thing I could do about it.

She put her feet up on the table and lifted her hips, sliding the white bikini bottoms down her thighs. Then she spread her legs, and I could see her cunt, shapely and bulbous, the dark hair trimmed. My whole body responded, wanting to climb inside her somehow, bury myself there. My cock knew exactly what it wanted, even if my head was telling me no. She leaned up on one elbow with a smile, using her other hand to reach down and open her lips, showing me the pink inside.

"Oh, God," I groaned, grabbing for my cock. I couldn't help it.

"Let me see, too." She nodded toward the hand kneading my boxers. I flushed, but I pulled them down, my erection springing free, and I couldn't help noticing how it was aiming directly at my stepsister's glistening cunt. I watched her hand move between her legs, rubbing her clit.

I knew it was a clit, I just hadn't ever seen a real one before. I'd seen pictures, up close pictures even, but this was entirely different from looking at a magazine, and my cock knew it. It was leading me toward the table as I watched her rub herself. She breathed harder, her eyes half closed, her feet up on the table and her legs spread wide.

"Dawnie," I whispered, nearing the edge of the table and looking down at her. "I want to look at it."

She smiled, using both hands and reaching down to open herself up for me. Oh, God, it was just like in the picture, only this was real. I bent down to take a peep, my gaze caressing the delicate folds and creases of her, dipping down to that lovely dark hole, where I felt like if I stared long enough, I could just get lost. I realised I could smell her. This was the smell of cunt! Tangy, a little musky. I could actually feel the heat of it against my face.

"I'm so randy," she murmured, slipping one of her fingers into the hole as I watched. That's where my cock would go, I thought, and it jumped in my hand as if to say, "Hell yes! Come on, man!" I stood, swallowing hard. So quiet, it was almost a sigh, she said, "I'm just going to rub myself off, okay?"

I nodded, watching her finger fuck herself, listening to the sloppy wet noises she made. My cock felt three times its normal size, like I could split the world open with it. As I began to pump it, I was actually surprised my hand could reach around it, that's how huge it felt. Dawn was moaning, using one hand on her cunt, the other pulling and tugging at her nipples.

My hand moved faster, and I could see her eyes half-open, looking down between her legs. I wondered if she was staring at my cock, and if she liked what she saw. Did girls like looking at us as much as we liked looking at them? I stroked the shaft, squeezing the tip, slick with pre-cum. My cock was pointed directly at her cunt, less than a foot away.

"Faster, David," she whispered, still frigging herself, her whole body moving with it, her hips rolling on the table. "Wank it faster. I want to see."

I did, shuttling my hand up and down, watching her flesh move under her hands, her lips swollen, the pinkness moving toward red. It matched the head of my cock, which was so red now it was almost purple as I stroked it. I could feel it building—it wouldn't be long. She was making these little noises in her throat, "uh, uh, uh" over and over, her head rolling from side to side.

"Ohhhhhh fuck!" Her eyes opened to look at me. "I'm gonna come!"

I groaned, pumping my cock furiously now, watching her come. She moaned and gasped, her whole body shuddering.

"Oh bloody hell!" I felt my own climax beginning. She slipped her feet off the table and scooted to the edge, grabbing my pulsing cock in her hand. That was more than enough to send me over, but then she pointed my spurting cock directly at her cunt. I groaned and jerked against her, shooting jets of hot, sticky cum onto her mound, watching as thick, ropey strands of it clung to her pubic hair, and some even dribbled down between her lips. I watched its descent, fascinated, my cock still throbbing in my hand.

When I was spent, she smiled, lifting her hand to her mouth. I watched, caught somewhere between horror and fascination, as she licked my cum off her hand.

"We taste good together, baby brother." She smiled.

I tucked my traitorous cock back into my boxers, flushing with embarrassment now. "Dawn... what are we doing?"

"I don't know." She slipped off the edge of the table. She turned to pick up her bikini bottoms that had fallen to the floor and my cock jumped in spite of the fact that it had just been sated. She turned and kissed me on the cheek, chaste, like a sister would, still bollock naked. "But don't you want to do it again?"

I shook my head no, but there were other, more treacherous parts of me that were saying "Yes!" with a great deal of vigour and enthusiasm.

Chapter Two

Mum knocked on my door for the third time that morning, and I groaned, covering my head with the pillow.

"David, c'mon now!"

"Okay!" I called, my voice muffled, hiding from the sun that was starting to peek through my window. I didn't want to face them. I didn't want to face anyone. Thinking about what happened yesterday made me want to stay under my pillow for just about forever.

I rolled over and tucked the pillow behind my head, staring up at the ceiling. How was I going to sit across the same breakfast table from her, considering what had happened on that table less than twenty-four hours ago? With Mum and Dad sitting right there? I swallowed hard, putting my arm over my eyes. Maybe if I just pretended nothing happened—and avoided Dawn. It was time to call my mates and see if there was somewhere I could hang all day—for the next two weeks.

I rolled out of bed, opening my door and looking down the hall. I could hear Mum wittering on downstairs to Dad about something. Dawn's door was closed. Grabbing a flannel and a towel out of the closet, I locked the door to the toilet with a relieved sigh. I started the shower running and cleaned my teeth while the water got hot. When I went to put my toothbrush back, I saw something white on the floor.

"Oh, bugger me," I whispered as I picked it up—a pair of Dawn's knickers! I sat on the toilet and stared at them. They were plain white with a little lace edging. The water running in the shower was hot enough to create steam now, but I ignored it, turning her knickers inside out and touching the gusset. They still felt damp! I looked around, as if someone could possibly see me, and lifted them to my nose.

Oh my God—that was the smell of my stepsister's cunt! My cock jumped in response, and I remembered in living, vivid colour the sight and sound and smell of my stepsister finger-fucking herself on the table downstairs. With that image, coupled with the wet, pungent knickers against my nose, my cock went into a full betrayal and tented my boxers. A knock on the door made me jump and I nearly screamed like a girl.

"David!" It was Dawn. I threw her knickers on the floor like they were on fire.

"What?"

"Hurry up in there, ya git!"

"Naff off!" I hoped my voice wasn't trembling as much as the rest of me. I got into the shower and finished as quickly as I could, not because of Dawn's insistence but because I wanted to get out of the house. Dad was at the table reading the paper.

He looked up when I skidded into the kitchen, heading for the Weetabix. "I set aside the jobs section for you, Davey." He tapped the folded up paper next to him.

"Ta," I said through a mouthful. I was eating them out of the box.

"A spoon and bowl?" Mum put them in front of me, giving me a look.

"Ta," I said again, pouring them in. Mum handed me the milk and I splashed some on, sitting across from Dad and shovelling cereal in as fast as I could, hoping to be done before Dawn came down.

Mum sat back down at the table next to Dad, folding her serviette in her lap and eating her toast. She always sat with her leg curled under her like that, and it occurred to me that Dawn often did, too.

"Any interviews?" Dad asked from behind the paper.

I shook my head, chewing fast and swallowing. "Not yet. I'm going to ring Will today and see if he can get me in over there."

I heard Dawn on the stairs and I choked on my cereal as she came around the corner. She had on the same white bikini she had been wearing yesterday.

Mum looked up and raised an eyebrow. "A bit parky to be wearing that out, isn't it?"

"It's my holiday," Dawn reminded her, sitting down next to me and curling her leg under her just like Mum. She reached into the middle of the table for a piece of toast and began spreading it with blackcurrant jam. I could see the way her arse and thighs spread on the chair, and I remembered how she had been spread out on the table. This very table.

Dawn sprang up and flounced over to the cupboard, taking out a box of Frosted Shreddies, and said over her shoulder with her mouth still full of toast: "I'm going to get a suntan even if it kills me."

"It might just." Dad lowered his paper and eyed my stepsister's attire. I was eyeing it too, as if I hadn't gotten enough of it yesterday. "You aren't really going out in that— even in the yard—I hope?"

Dawn rolled her eyes. "I thought I would just lie on the table and sun myself in here!" She looked directly at me, smiling as she filled her bowl full of cereal.

I felt my cheeks getting hot and I lifted my bowl, drinking my milk to hide my face.

"Mum, can I borrow your black jumper?" Dawn asked through a mouthful of Frosted Shreddies, coming to sit next to me again.

"Where are you going?" Mum handed me a piece of toast as I reached for it.

Dawn smiled. "Ken gave me a quick snog at the pub last weekend—I think he fancies me. Laurie and I are going back up there tonight."

"Alone?" Dad asked. "You should take David with you. He's eighteen now."

Dawn and I looked at each other, aghast, and we both said, "No!" at the same time.

"Mum!" we both exclaimed, looking at her and back at each other. I noticed a bit of milk dribbling down Dawn's chin, and I flashed on yesterday's tabletop adventure and the delicious sight of my cum dribbling down her slit. I averted my eyes, looking at the toast in my hand, but not before I saw her smirk at me and stretch her tongue out to lick at the white stuff.

"Mum, he's such a baby! I can't have him tagging along with me!" My stepsister nudged me in the side with her elbow, and I watched as her breast flesh shifted with the movement.

"Dawn, stop your whingeing!" Mum stood up and began to clear the table. "You can borrow my jumper, and you don't have to take your brother."

My stepsister and I both let out our breath. I got up, edging around her chair. Dad looked over his paper at me.

"Where are you off to?" He tapped the jobs section of the paper on the table.

I froze and saw that Dawn was looking at me, still munching on her cereal. She had the same mischievous look in her eyes that she had yesterday, and it made my stomach drop.

"I thought I'd ring Will—" I started, but his look stopped me.

"David, do I need to remind you that it is imperative that you find a job? Everyone here in this family contributes. I work. Your mother works. Dawn works."

I snorted. "Right, tramping it up at the health club, that's working."

Dawn stuck her tongue out at me but she was giving me the finger under the table where Dad and Mum couldn't see. I used my middle finger to scratch my forehead, looking pointedly at her.

"A job is a job." My father held the paper out to me. "And I suggest you find one."

"All right, keep your hair on!" I sighed, coming over to pick it up.

Mum called over from where she was washing up. "David, don't speak back to your father!"

I nudged Dawn's chair on my way by, taking the paper and storming up to my room. I turned on my radio—loud—

and waited for them all to leave. Mum poked her head in the door and saw the paper still sitting on my desk.

She frowned at it, and then at me. "David, please try."

"I am trying!"

She came over to the bed and put her hand on my forehead, like she was checking for a fever. "You've been awfully stroppy lately. What is it?"

Your daughter is trying to book me a first class ticket to hell, I thought. I shrugged and rolled away from her, going to the window, and there was Dawn, lying out on the lounge chair, like some surreal deja-vu. Her face was obscured by a book, but I could see the rest of her well enough.

"I'll find something, Mum. Give me a chance."

"See you tonight." She pulled the door closed. I hadn't moved from the window—I couldn't. Dawn was adjusting the straps on her bikini again, her breasts moving with the material, and I was remembering seeing her dark pink nipples for the first time. My cock seemed to like the thought, because it was starting to make my jeans more uncomfortable. "Oh, and David—behave!"

I turned my face to the door, incredulous, but she was gone. Behave? Hell, I was trying—I was really trying—but there was a very pointed part of me that wanted to be very, very naughty. Dawn was putting more lotion on now, slathering it over her belly, the tops of her breasts, the insides of her thighs. She parted her legs for the latter, and I remembered how she looked laid out like that, all wide open and frigging herself until she came. Fuck. I was doomed.

I spent the whole morning in my room, listening to music and trying to concentrate on finding a job. Dawn spent all morning on the lounge chair. I know because I spent fifteen minutes out of every sixty standing at the window, rubbing my cock and telling myself I was trying to get my erection to disappear. It was useless. I couldn't think about anything now but my stepsister's sweet, pink cunt.

I crept downstairs when I got hungry. A fizzy pop and a bag of crisps were handy and I was starting back to my room with them when Dawn came in the back door. She smiled and winked as she came toward me.

"I have a question for you." She stopped in front of me and looked up. My eyes were on her breasts. I swallowed hard.

"What?"

"Do you think it's working?" She reached behind her neck and untied the thin white straps that held up her bikini top. My jaw dropped as she lowered them and the two small triangles covering her breasts. There they were again— heavy, creamy white flesh topped with a brownish-pink nipple apiece that pointed straight towards me. My eyes flicked up to her face, and I saw that mischievous Dawnie smile playing on her lips.

"Can you see any lines?" She lifted her breasts, turning to the side a little.

"Dawn, quit it." I cleared my throat and moved to go past her. "This is so wrong I don't even know where to start."

"I'm serious!" She edged around me and stopped in my way again.

"So am I."

"Don't be mean," she purred, turning her back to me and pulling her bikini bottoms up so they rode between her arse cheeks. She looked over her shoulder at me. "Do you see lines?"

"No." I stared at the full, round globes of her arse. "I think you're going to have to stay out there longer."

"Oh, hell," she muttered, turning back around. Her breasts were still exposed and they swayed a little when she moved. "Ooo, crisps!" She snatched the bag out of my hand, opening them and heading toward the back door.

"Hey!"

"So come and get 'em," she teased, waving the bag and winking. "Oh, David—it's hot out here. Would you get me an iced lolly? Please?"

I sighed, turning back toward the fridge and fulfilling her request. When I walked outside, she was back in the lounge chair, her top done up again, munching on the crisps.

"Let's trade," I said, holding out the lolly and pointing at the crisps. She handed me the bag and I gave her the lolly, watching her unwrap it as I opened my Coke. I sat at the patio table, stuffing crisps into my mouth and washing them down with sweet carbonation. It was enough to make my eyes water, but if that didn't do it, then watching Dawn suck her lolly would have.

It was pink and it made her lips and tongue turn colour as she licked it. She turned it around and around in her mouth, making little happy noises. She saw me looking at her and really started putting on a show, trailing her tongue from the base to the tip, swirling it around and then—holy fuck! She took the whole iced lolly into her mouth, all the way to the stick! I choked on my fizzy drink, feeling my cock aching.

"You like that?" she asked after she'd pulled it from her throat, wet and pink and glistening.

I nodded, not trusting my voice.

"Have you ever had a girl do that?"

I shook my head, watching her twirl the lolly against her pinkened tongue.

"Do you want to?" She swung her legs off the side of the lounge chair and sat up. "I love doing it. Sliding a big, thick prick into my mouth. I can take a lot 'til I gag on it." She showed me, with the lolly, just how much she could take again, all the way to the stick.

"I'm not saying I mind gagging." She grinned. "You should gag a little on a bloke's cock. They like it. Makes them think they're much too big for your tiny little mouth."

Oh, holy hell. My cock was raging in my pants now, and I felt like I was in some sort of a trance, listening to her, watching her. The thought of my cock in her mouth was making me loopy, and the thought that she might gag a little on it? Christ! I shook my head, as if to clear it, standing up.

"I need to look for a job." I wasn't sure if I was reminding her or myself. I made it all the way to the living room before she caught up with me. She didn't have the lolly anymore, but her mouth was pink and sticky with it as she smiled up at me.

"You don't need to look anymore." She pressed herself against me. I could feel her sun-warmed skin, like she was a little running heater.

"What?" I wasn't thinking clearly at all. She ran her hand up the inside leg of my jeans to my crotch, cupping and rubbing her hand there. I gritted my teeth, willing myself not to respond. I was already as hard as a rock.

"You don't need to look for a job." She sank to her knees in front of me. Oh God. My stepsister on her knees, looking up at me while she unzipped my jeans, was just too much. "I'm going to give you one."

She freed my cock, and I leaned back against the wall to have something to hold me up. Her pink tongue was licking her lips, wetting them, as she began to stroke me.

"Dawn, no!"

"A nice, long blowjob." She kissed the tip. "Isn't that what you really want?"

Once her mouth opened and took me in, I was lost. I had never felt anything so incredible in my life! Her mouth was actually still cold but soon warmed up as she showed me with her lips and tongue just exactly what she had done outside to the lolly. I had imagined what it would be like to feel a girl's mouth on my cock, but my imagination hadn't gone nearly far enough.

Her tongue painted liquid velvet strokes all over the tip, using her hand to hold the skin down tight. She bobbed her head on it then, taking more and more with every motion, working her way down to the base. Her mouth was like a tight, wet core of heat all around me, and she never took her eyes off mine as she sucked, deeper and deeper.

I watched as I disappeared into her mouth until—for fuck's sake! She was gagging—my stepsister was gagging on my cock! Her head moved faster and faster, still, in spite of her discomfort. I felt my knees go weak and they started to buckle. Dawn stopped then, her mouth gone from pink to red, now.

"Let's get more comfy." She tugged at my cock as she stood. She used it as a leash, leading me with her as she moved to the sofa. I watched her hips sway, the way the bikini bottoms hugged her and rode up a little. She pushed me down and pulled my jeans the rest of the way off, and then my boxers, too. She knelt between my legs, batting at my cock with her fingertips, her nails grazing the shaft lightly.

"How do you like it so far, little brother?" Her mouth was inches from the tip. I could feel her breath, and could even smell it, the cherry pink lolly. I wondered if she still tasted like it, and found myself wanting to kiss her. That seemed so much more wrong than anything we'd done, somehow.

"Dawn…" I reached out to touch her hair and tuck it behind her ear.

"Don't say no." She shook her head and smiled, moving her mouth back over me now, covering me and taking me in. I groaned, moving my hips with her, I couldn't help it.

"Oh, hell," I moaned. "This is so wrong!" Her mouth was heaven, slick, hot heaven up and down on me, her fingernails grazing my balls now.

She came up for air, still stroking me. "That's why it feels so good," she whispered, her eyes on mine. She was right, and I knew it. Aside from the physical sensation, which was unbelievable, it was also the fact that Dawn was my stepsister, and that we were both round the twist to even be thinking about this, let alone actually doing it on our parents' sofa.

She went back to work on me, and I could feel my pent-up lust for her ready to explode. I reached my hand down, tentative at first, feeling her breast through her bikini top. She smiled around my cock, still working it in and out of her mouth, and she didn't miss a beat as she reached around and undid it, exposing her flesh to me. Oh my God, she was incredible.

I rolled her nipples in my fingers as she sucked me and that made her move up and down faster and moan around my cock, sending vibrations down my shaft. Her tits swayed as she moved, brushing up against my thighs. I put my hand on the top of her head, pressing her down a little until she gagged. I groaned, and she smiled again around my shaft, still not letting up. I wasn't going to last much longer, and I think she knew it.

That's when she stopped, using her tongue to roll around tip, slipping under my foreskin to reach the sensitive flesh underneath, making me buck and groan against her. She stood then, slipping her bikini bottoms down and untying her bikini top, letting them both drop to the floor. Then she spread her pussy lips open, moving between my legs so I could see her.

"Do you want to touch me?" She put one foot up on my thigh so her lips were slightly open. I nodded, reaching my hand out and brushing it over the soft skin of her vulva, stroking in the direction of her trimmed bush, all the hairs seeming to direct my fingers between her lips. I spread her with one hand, using my thumb and forefinger, peering into the pink. The closest I'd come to a cunt was a brief feel down Sara Bailey's knickers in a dark bedroom at some party, just enough to feel hair and wetness before she pushed me away.

Dawn was wide open to me, in full daylight, and I took my time exploring her, running my fingers through the soft folds of flesh, parting them, watching them glisten. She moaned when my fingers brushed her clit, and I stopped there, pulling the little hood back so I could see it, just a tiny little thing. It amazed me that something so small could give her such pleasure, but it was clear it did from the way she rocked her hips and her nostrils flared and her head went back when I rubbed it.

"I want you to lick it." Dawn ran a hand through my hair. I looked up at her, surprised. She smiled and nudged me aside, lying down on the sofa and putting one foot up on the back and dangling the other towards the floor. I knelt down and stretched out between her legs, breathing in the smell of her. I hesitated—I didn't know what to do.

"Here." She looked down, opening herself with her fingers and pointing to her clit, stroking it with her fingernail as I watched. "Right here. Put your tongue—"

I didn't need a second invitation. I edged her fingers out of the way, rubbing my tongue over the little button, back and forth. She tasted tangy, strong, and I could smell her sweat from lying out in the sun all morning.

She gasped, rolling her hips a little as my tongue mashed against her, lapping and licking and swallowing the taste of her. It stayed in my throat, thick and rich. I watched her belly quiver, her breasts heaving, her breath coming faster as I moved my face between her thighs, my tongue exploring the sweet ridges and folds.

"Put your fingers in me." She bucked her hips. I slipped a finger down, between her slit, searching for that dark little entrance I'd seen yesterday.

Dawn squealed, her eyes flying open. "Higher." She reached her hand down and found mine, leading my fingers upward. I flushed, realizing that I must have been pressing against her anus. She moved against me and I could feel the soft, smooth walls inside of her. She started to rock, encouraging me to move my fingers in and out.

"Lick." She pointed to her clit. I did, my tongue moving over her flesh. She moaned, still moving her hips, and I pressed my fingers in her, trying to catch a rhythm between my lapping tongue and my plunging fingers. It felt a little like trying to walk and chew gum at the same time at first, but I got the hang of it. I knew for sure that I did when she hissed and grabbed at my hair, smashing my face between her legs.

"Oh, God," she moaned, and I could feel the muscles in her fanny tightening. I licked faster, looking up and seeing her pinching and pulling on her nipples. My cock was dripping pre-cum now, throbbing against the sofa, and I knew there would probably be a stain there, but I didn't care. She tasted so good, and the way she moved and sounded and felt was almost enough to make me come myself.

"Oh fuck, David!" she cried, breathless, shaking. "Oooooo make me come, baby brother!"

I grunted, moving my whole head as I licked her, plunging my fingers deep. She strained against me, rolling back and forth, making those same little noises she had yesterday, that little, "uh, uh, uh" until she stiffened and shuddered under me. I could feel the muscles inside fluttering against my fingers when she came, her cunt wetter than ever now.

She reached for me as I sat up, grabbing onto my shirt and pulling me on top of her. My cock was pressed against her cunt, all wet and slippery, and I groaned. She kissed me, plunging her tongue deep into my mouth, exploring the insides of my cheeks, licking my teeth, her hands running up under my shirt and squeezing my nipples, making me jump.

"Dammit, Dawn," I murmured against her mouth, feeling her hand working my cock between her legs, aiming me. I moaned. "Ohhh fuck, no, we can't do this."

"We are doing this," she said. "I want to feel you inside me."

"Noooo," I groaned, sitting up and leaning back on the sofa, my eyes closed, panting. "Dawn, I can't. I just can't. You're my sister!"

She crawled across the sofa towards me on her hands and knees, her tits swaying prettily, licking her lips. "God, I love the taste of my cunt, don't you?"

I wiped my mouth with my hand, still wet with her juices. I could taste her, smell her, and my cock was a throbbing, weeping pulse between my legs, standing straight up and defying my better judgement. She stretched out next to me, reaching her hand out to stroke me. It was a lazy, easy motion, but I was beyond any edge I had ever known— I was that close.

"Did you like licking my cunt, baby brother?" She tilted her head up to look at me. Why did she keep calling me that? It was driving me crackers, forcing me to try to choose between my lust and my conviction. I couldn't forget for a moment that this was my stepsister—she wouldn't let me. And I was beginning to realise that it didn't matter, because lust was winning—it was kicking conviction's arse.

"Fuck, Dawn." I watched her hand on my shaft. Her arse was rising up, her feet swinging behind her. She was beautiful, and I wanted her. God help me, but I wanted her. "You still taste so good in my mouth. I could lick your cunt forever."

"I might take you up on that." She grinned. "But first, I think you have an itch you need scratched." She grazed her fingernails over the head of my cock, tickling the frenulum. I groaned. She moved in, pressing her breasts against my thigh and taking my cock fully into her mouth.

When she came up on me, she pressed herself up with her arms and kissed me for a minute, the words husky and thick in her throat, "I'm going to suck you until you come in my mouth, and I'm going to swallow every last drop. Are you ready?"

"Yes!" I pressed her head down to my lap. "Oh, God, Dawnie, suck me off."

She settled back down into my lap, nuzzling and nosing my cock, murmuring sweetness around it as she began to suck, holding the skin down tight with her fingers at the base and using just her mouth and throat, up and down the shaft. I knew it wouldn't take long and so did she, her tongue wrapped around, her hand cupping my balls as she worked, determined.

Her arse rose up in the air and I watched her tits moving as she swayed, reaching my hand out to cup one, pulling at the nipple. She moaned, moving faster, and I liked that, so I squeezed and kneaded her flesh some more. I was trying hard to hold back, wanting it to go on forever, watching my stepsister's head bobbing up and down in my lap, seeing her sweet, rounded arse moving like she was fucking some invisible cock back there.

It was that thought—and more, the thought of my own cock sliding into that smooth, velvet pink hole—that sent me over. I growled, thrusting into her throat, and I heard her gag a little and that made it even better, my cum shooting in shuddering waves into her mouth. She was making little noises, and I heard her swallowing, swallowing, I could see her throat working, her eyes wide, her mouth stretched over my cock.

"Ohhhhh God!" I bucked with the last of it, my hand in her hair, pulling her back, my cock just sensitive, throbbing heat between my legs now. Dawn sat up, leaning back against the arm of the sofa, licking her lips.

"Mmmmm, I love your cock, baby brother." She nudged me with her bare foot. I looked down at it, slumping now, spent. Conviction was winning again, and I glanced over at her, shaking my head.

"Quit calling me that." I stood up and reached for my jeans and boxers.

"Blimey!" She stood and gathered up her bikini. "You know you were arching for it! Now you're all high and mighty? Knob off!"

She stormed up the stairs and I heard her slam her bedroom door. I stood there, holding my jeans in my hand and looking at the couch. I was right, there was a stain on the side that I was going to have to clean up before Mum saw, or we'd get nicked.

Oh, hell. I knew Dawn was right. I was off my damned head, but I wanted exactly what she had given me—and more. So very much more.

Chapter Three

First there was the trouser suit—white with blue trim. Awful looking thing, but her arse looked great in it, I had to admit. Then there was the jeans and jumper combination. I liked how tight the jumper was across her breasts, how her jeans moulded over her flesh. That was my favourite until the red leather skirt and white blouse sailed by my bedroom door, the perfect combination of low cut, hip-hugging, and up-the-thigh-riding perfection.

I was lying on my bed, pretending to read while watching Dawn move back and forth between her room and the washroom. Every time she passed, she was wearing something different. Once in a while, she would pause in my doorway and ask, "This one?" Most of the time, she wouldn't even stop to listen to my response.

"I like that one!" I called, hearing her in the washroom again. She came around the corner, and I saw she was wearing red high heels with it, too. Hot. Definitely hot.

"This one? Are you sure?" She turned slightly, showing me her behind.

I frowned. Considering my own response to her outfit, I could imagine the general masculine consensus in the pub. "Maybe not," I said, changing my mind. "I'd go with the trouser suit."

She made a face. "It's too dowdy—I look like mum in that. This is a date, not a job interview."

"So?" I sat up and looked at her body filling out the clothes. "It's—it's sophisticated. Guys like that."

She snorted. "Guys like skin. I think I'm showing enough, don't you?"

I cleared my throat. "You've got a ladder in your tights." I pointed to it, high up on her thigh. It must have started near the gusset and worked its way down.

"Bugger!" she swore, twisting to look. "Oh, hell. I just won't wear any."

I watched as she kicked off her heels, pulling her skirt up to her waist and sliding the tights down over her knickers. The fake tan material revealed the creamy, smooth white skin of my stepsister's thighs and calves as she worked them down. Her knickers were red, too, with white lace edging, riding up into the crack of her arse.

"Dawn!" I exclaimed, sounding shocked, or rather trying to sound shocked.

She grinned back at me, the tights in her hand, slipping her heels back on. "What? It's not anything you haven't seen, right?"

"What if mum comes up?" I hissed, watching her wiggle her skirt back down her hips.

Dawn glanced toward the stairway. "She wouldn't think anything." Smiling at me, she advanced into the room, standing by me near the bed. "After all, we're brother and sister, right? That would be..." she put her foot up between my legs on the bed, nudging my crotch with her shoe. "Wrong... wouldn't it?"

I was staring straight up her skirt, past the swell of her thighs, right at the swollen gusset of her knickers. "Dawn, you can be really crude sometimes," I said, pushing her leg away and standing up. "Clear off!"

She sighed, tossing her thick blonde hair over her shoulder. She paused to look into the mirror over my bureau. "I like this one." She turned sideways again, assessing her profile.

"Yeah." I leaned against the wall with a sigh, crossing my arms over my chest. "Me, too."

"I knew you did." She turned back to me, looking chuffed with herself. "Ken will like it."

"That twit?" I tossed myself back on my bed, grabbing my book and pretending to read.

"He is not!"

I looked at her over my book. "I just think you should mention it."

She looked over her shoulder at me, narrowing her eyes. "Mention what?"

"You might want to let him know that he's really missed."

She turned fully to me now, her lips thin, her arms crossed. "David, don't be obtuse."

I grinned, turning over on my belly, dismissing her. "Since, you know, some village somewhere is being totally deprived of their idiot."

She made an angry sound in her throat, and I waited for her to tackle me, but she didn't. Instead, she walked out and slammed my door hard enough to shake the wall.

I listened to her go down the stairs and heard the murmur of her talking to Mum and Dad. So she was going out to the pub—dressed like a tart. Still, why should it be any concern of mine? What the hell was wrong with me?

I went back to reading my book, but I didn't realise how intently I was paying attention to what was going on downstairs until I heard her best friend, Laurie's, voice for a moment, and then it was quiet again after the front door closed. That was when I stopped grinding my teeth and my jaw relaxed for the first time in an hour. I rubbed at it—it ached—and for some reason all I could imagine was what Dawn looked like with her foot wedged against my crotch.

* * * *

"David?"

I woke up with a grunt, hearing my name being hissed from beside the bed. It was dark, but I could make out her outline in the moonlight coming through the window. She was on her hands and knees, crawling toward me.

"Dawn?" I felt her find the bed with a thud.

"Ow." She whimpered.

"Christ!" I reached for her, groping in the dark. My hand found her arm, helping her up into the bed. "What are you doing?"

"Ta," she said, thanking me. I could smell the alcohol on her, now. "It's a long way when you're legless."

"Shhhh!" I looked toward my door. I was listening for Mum or Dad, but didn't hear them. "C'mon, let's get you to bed."

"That's where I am." She crawled up against me in the dark and pressed me down, snuggling up against my bare chest. "Hey, you sleep naked! When did you start that?"

"Since I was fourteen," I whispered. "Keep your voice down, Dawn."

"I am." She kissed my shoulder. "You feel good."

"Okay."I tried to untangle her limbs from mine. "You are pretty well lashed, and I think this is a bad idea. C'mon, let's go."

"Noooo!" She slid her bare foot up the inside of my calf. She'd lost her heels somewhere, I noticed, but I could feel the skirt and blouse pressed against me, her body full and warm underneath, flushed from the alcohol. "Don't make me go."

"I think you'd better." I tried to sit, but she was clinging to me too tightly.

"I'll scream," she whispered into my ear, her breath hot against my neck.

"You will not." I edged my way out from under her.

I heard her intake of breath and knew she really meant to do it. Panicked, I rolled onto her, finding her mouth with my hand in the dark and pressing it there, hard.

"Button it!" I hissed, feeling her wiggling and squirming underneath me. Her skirt was riding high up and I could feel her bare thighs against mine, her skin like velvet.

"Unbutton it," she murmured when I moved my hand away from her mouth, her fingers working her blouse from top to bottom between us. She pulled her shirt open, sliding her breasts against my chest, back and forth. Her nipples were hard, her breath hot with alcohol against my face, her hands roaming over my back.

"Dawn," I whispered, and I knew she could feel my cock growing against her leg, insisting that my denial was empty. "Please, let's just—"

"I've been thinking about this all night." Her hands slid down my arse and she ground her hips up and wrapped her legs around me. "I can't think about anything but your prick, little brother—how big and hard you get for me and how much I want you."

I groaned softly against her neck, my cock finding its way between her legs somehow, pressed right up to the soft, satiny red gusset of her knickers as she rocked herself beneath me.

"Please, David." She was reaching her hand down between her legs, and I could feel her pulling her knickers aside, exposing her wetness.

"No," I whispered, feeling helpless as she worked my cock with her hand, rubbing it up and down her slick folds of flesh. "No, no, God, please, no."

"Oh yes!" She rubbed the head of my cock right over her clit. "Yes, yes." Her hand slanted my cock toward the hot little target she was now aiming for, rocking her hips up, determined to put me inside of her. I gritted my teeth, pulling back and rolling to the side. She followed me, kissing me in the dark, sucking at my lips, my tongue, and I knew for certain that it was tequila she had been drinking, the taste unmistakable in her mouth.

"Don't you want to fuck me?" she whispered against my cheek, rolling her hips and trapping my cock between us.

"It isn't about want," I gasped as she sat up on me. In the moonlight, her hair and eyes were like silver, her skin like milk, and she reached between her breasts to unhook her bra, spilling her generous flesh for my view. Then she reached for my hands, cupping them over her breasts as she slid her knickers up and down against my shaft, the dampness spreading.

"Oh yes," she whispered as I began to give in, kneading her flesh in my hands, thumbing her nipples. "It's all about want, baby." She reached between us, wrapping her hand around me and saying, "I want, I want, I want." She punctuated each "want" with a tug on my cock that made me gasp.

"We can't." I grabbed her hips and slid her up away from my cock. I could smell her cunt as I edged her up my chest and I wanted it. Just the smell of it now made me drool like some Pavlovian response. I shoved her leather skirt up higher, sliding my fingers under the elastic of her knickers and exploring her flesh. She was soaking wet.

"You want to lick my cunt, baby brother?" I felt her hands sliding past mine, rubbing herself.

"Stop calling me that."

She rubbed her wet fingers over my mouth, giving me a taste of her. I licked my lips, moaning, and then I licked hers, slipping her knickers aside and plunging my tongue into her flesh. Her sigh was a relieved "Finally!" and she moved her cunt against me, her hips rocking in my hands.

She tasted sweet tonight, her juices coating my chin as I focused my tongue on her little clit. I could see her pulling at her nipples in the moonlight and her toes were curling against my sides. My cock was poking the sheet straight up and I rocked my hips, remembering how my stepsister's cunt felt rubbing against me. I wanted to be inside of her—I could feel it like a gnawing hunger, growing more intense with every encounter.

"Oh fuck, baby, lick my cunt!" She moaned softly and rotated her hips in my hands, forcing my tongue into little circles over her clit. Her moans kept getting louder the faster I licked, and her hands gripped the headboard, rocking it against the wall as she moved. The more turned on she got, the more she said, and while my cock was drooling at her words, my brain was screaming that if she got much louder, we were going to get nicked.

"Dawn!" I pushed her hips back, my face soaked with her. "You have to be quiet!"

"Ohhh, I don't give a toss!" She pressed her hips forward again, searching for my mouth with her cunt.

"You will when Dad comes in here and turns on the light!"

She was wiggling in my hands, the leather skirt shifting and moving over her hips. It was hard to hold her still, and I could smell her all over me, permeating my senses—it was intoxicating, and I felt more drunk with her now than she'd been when she crawled into my room. I wanted to eat her little cunt until she came all over my face. I wanted it so much my cock was in agony with the desire.

I said the only thing I could think of. "If you can't be quiet, then keep your mouth busy, all right?"

She giggled, and the sound thrilled me for some reason—the girlish little giggle of my stepsister as she sat on my chest and I licked at her juices coating my mouth.

"You want me to suck you off, Davey?"

My cock seemed to be lunging toward her voice. She was sliding out of my hands, turning herself over on me. She stood over me on the bed and slipped her knickers down, stepping out of them before straddling my head, this time facing my aching crotch.

"Is this what you wanted?" She swiped the sheet away and wrapped her hand around my shaft. "You want me to keep my mouth busy all over this hard cock?" She began licking it, using her tongue to paint saliva all over the tip.

I groaned, gripping her arse in my hands as her mouth worked me up and down. I still couldn't believe how incredible it was to have a girl's mouth wrapped around my cock. I forgot about everything the minute she started to suck me, all my attention centred on the exquisite anguish between my thighs.

"Oh, God." I moaned when she used her tongue around my foreskin again, tickling the sensitive skin underneath. I heard her giggle with her tongue rolling around my shaft.

"Shhhh, David," she whispered, teasing me, and I felt her breath over my crotch. "You have to be quiet, remember?"

"Right," I said, remembering with a jolt. God, it was hard to concentrate on anything with her mouth moving up and down my flesh like that.

"Don't want to wake Mum and Dad." She came up on me, rolling her tongue around the tip before sinking back down again. Mum and Dad? Who are they, I wondered, shuddering and closing my eyes as I thrust up into her throat. I couldn't help it—the heat of her mouth was irresistible—I didn't care anymore that it was my stepsister's mouth I was fucking, that this was unquestionably wrong in so many ways. I didn't even care about getting caught, in that moment. All I cared about was the wonderful feeling of her mouth sliding wetly up and down over my cock.

"Hey, little brother," she murmured around the swollen head of my shaft, wiggling her arse over me. "You're forgetting something."

Oh, right. It wasn't that I'd completely forgotten about Dawn's wet cunt spread inches from my face in the darkness—I could smell her and still taste her in my throat. The thought of putting my mouth there made my cock stiffen more than I thought possible. I was just... distracted.

Dawn "mmmm'd" around the shaft in her mouth when I began probing between her lips. It was dark and my perspective was skewed—things were shifted and upside down. I tried to find the right direction, her swollen folds of flesh like a slick, wet labyrinth that I was trying to trace with my tongue. Dawn spread her lips open and rubbed her clit, encouraging me to find it. I followed her fingers, locating the hard little button of flesh and flicking my tongue there.

She sighed and rolled her hips, whispering, "Faster," against my cock head. I obliged, now that I'd found the right spot, working my tongue over and over it. I loved the way she tasted, the way she pushed down against me when she wanted it harder. It was difficult to concentrate on giving pleasure while receiving it, but if I forgot, Dawn would remind me with her hips, grinding them into my face. I would have happily licked her forever, but I wasn't going to last that long.

In fact, I was rather close. All her sucking and tugging, her body half-naked and writhing on me, the little sounds she was starting to make that I was beginning to associate with her being ready to come, that little "uh, uh, uh," were all pushing me toward the brink. I could feel it swelling like some incredible tidal wave rushing toward shore.

"Come for me!" She stroked my cock against her cheek. "Come all over my face, baby brother." I gave a low grunt and did as she asked, pumping my hips into her hand, feeling her mouth over my cock trying to catch wave after wave of my cum with her waiting tongue.

The knock on my door nearly propelled Dawn off me when I jumped, but I grabbed her hips just in time. My heart was in my throat, and my voice was hoarse, thank God, a little sleepy sounding in my dazed confusion when I called out, "Yes?"

"David?" It was my mother's voice, right outside the door. Oh, sodding hell! We were in trouble, now. Dawn sank down flat onto me and I pulled the sheet up to my neck, all just in time, too, as my mother opened my door a crack.

"Yeah, Mum? What time is it?" I mumbled, my heart still hammering like a race horse in my chest. She didn't have the hall light on, and that was good, or she would have seen the shape of my stepsister lying on me under the sheet, I was sure. I could only see her outline, and I assumed she could only see mine.

"Did you hear your sister come in?"

"No." I tried to keep my voice from shaking.

"Sorry to wake you, sweetheart," she said. "It's just late, that's all."

She pulled the door closed, and I heard her moving toward the loo. Dawn let out a sigh of relief, throwing the sheet off. Neither of us said a word, frozen in place until we heard the toilet flush and we listened to Mom pad back down the hall and close her bedroom door.

"You need to go to bed." My voice was really trembling. Even my hands were shaking. Holy fuck! The realization that my mother knocking on my door in the middle of the night could have turned out very differently just now hit me square in the chest. I could barely breathe.

"I will," Dawn whispered. "As soon as I come all over your face, little brother."

"God," I breathed, feeling her mouth back on my limp cock, feeling it responding to her tongue in spite of the fact that I'd just come minutes before. "We really shouldn't... Oh, fuck, Dawn!"

"Lick me!" She positioned herself over my face again, spreading herself with her fingers. And I did—God help me, I did, my blood still pumping adrenaline-compelled ice through my veins from the interruption by our Mum. I licked and sucked her cunt harder and faster than I ever had before, no more looking for the right spot or trying to figure out what to do. I just went after her like a nutter, lapping and sucking and swallowing the whole of her cunt.

Dawn was breathing hard, whispering, "fuck, uh, uh, uh, fuck, fuck!" as I ate her. She remembered my cock then and put it back into her mouth, sucking me with all the earnest lust I seemed to be feeling, taking me to the hilt and gagging silently on my cock as she did and then taking some more. There was just no stopping it, no stopping us—we were doomed, and it felt like being sentenced to an eternity of ecstatic hell.

I felt her coming, her whole body tightening and releasing with it, bucking so hard I had to hold her arse in my hands and plaster my mouth over her slit, staying glued to her as she writhed against me.

She rolled off me, then, tumbling to the floor. I held my breath, sure the noise would bring Mum running down the hall, but it didn't.

"Jesus," Dawn whispered. "That was—"

I could feel it, too. It felt like I was floating somewhere near the ceiling.

"Go to bed, Dawn," I whispered. "Before we really do get caught."

She crawled toward the door, using the handle to steady herself as she stood.

"Goodnight, David." She still sounded as dazed as I felt.

"'Night."

She opened the door as quietly as she could. "Hey...I love you."

My head was too full of her, the blood beginning to return there. I didn't know what else to say. "I love you, too."

When she shut the door, I turned over in bed and pulled the pillow over my head to drown it all out. I ached all over, like I'd drunk a poison that was turning my insides to acid, but my throbbing cock was stiffening again, even now, at the thought of her. This was insane.

I rolled over and stared at the dull light of the moon on the ceiling. Everything had a silver sheen to it, like quicksilver, slippery and shifting. I closed my eyes, deciding to try to get some sleep. Maybe when I opened them again in the light of day, things would look clearer. It was all I could hope for.

Chapter Four

I spent the morning on the telephone ringing potential employers while Dawn moaned and groaned from the sofa that I was being too sodding loud. Mum had ripped her a new one at the breakfast table, after dragging her down in the first place. When they left for work, she crawled to the living room, probably because she couldn't make it all the way back upstairs, and between bouts of snoring, saw fit to berate me for even existing on the same planet.

I wasn't having much luck, anyway, although I did manage to schedule one interview later in the week, so I took a break and got myself a glass of milk and a couple of custard cremes . Hearing my stepsister groaning again, I dug to the back of the fridge and found an Irn-Bru—a bright orange fizzy drink. She was lying on her back on the sofa with an arm thrown over her eyes. Her shiny, pink robe had pulled apart a little, exposing her thigh and a little bit of pubic hair.

"Hey." I squatted down and tried to avoid looking between her legs, remembering last night. It wasn't easy. "I brought you some Irn-Bru. Great for hangovers."

She groaned but peeked out from under her arm at me. "Ta."

Blinking and squinting, she sat up, reaching for the drink. I opened it for her and handed it over, watching how her robe split apart even further, showing me the curve of her breasts, the roundness of her belly and thighs. I watched her swallowing, the way her throat moved, and couldn't seem to find my breath. She handed the empty bottle back to me.

"Ta, Davey," she murmured. "You're a love." She collapsed back onto the couch, her robe gaping now, and I found myself overcome with an urge to run my hands over her. I knew she wouldn't appreciate it, considering, and I was still fighting with my own demons. I grabbed a blanket off the back of the sofa and covered her instead.

Smiling, she mumbled, "I'm sorry I called you a fuckwit."

"What else are little brothers for?" I watched her turn away from the light, pulling the blanket with her.

I decided to give her a break from the noise and go sit out on the patio to finish looking at the paper. My stepsister was missing out on another perfect sun-bathing day, although there was more of a wind, and I had to struggle to keep my paper still. I sat and highlighted possibilities, but my mind wasn't on the task at hand anymore. All the blood had been diverted from my brain.

The sight of Dawn's pubic hair, even just a little exposed under her robe, made me remember how she tasted in my mouth. I still couldn't believe that the first cunt I ever tasted was my own stepsister's. The thought made me flush, with both shame and excitement. I closed my eyes, remembering the softness of her flesh against my tongue, the soft cries she made, that little "uh, uh, uh" before she came. It was like I was addicted to it, now. I couldn't seem to think about anything else.

I sighed, giving up on my paper, and walked over to the shed, my cock leading the way. I dug my favourite porn mag, *Naughty Bits,* out from under the wood pile, flipping it open to the page. There she was... lying on her tummy on the bed, her legs open, her cunt exposed for me. I flipped the page, and found that it was even more thrilling to me now, imagining that it was her brother coming in to disrupt her in this picture, now that things between Dawn and I were hotting up.

I'd thought she looked like my stepsister, and she did— but now I realised that her cunt was different. Dawn's was fuller, fleshier, thicker—and even more pink. My cock was aching now, and I undid my jeans and freed it, rubbing my thumb over the tip with a shiver.

I started wanking, my eyes on the sweet pink of her cunt. Now I knew what it felt like to touch one. I knew what it tasted like, what my fingers sounded like moving in and out of that hot, moist flesh. Now I wanted it more than ever.

When I flipped the page, I remembered that first morning she and I had been together. I could close my eyes and see her finger-fucking herself, her breasts trembling and shaking with the effort, her soft moans. My mind skipped forward to the first time I'd licked her, right there on the sofa she was inside asleep on, and the first time I'd felt her mouth wrapped around my cock.

My hand, moving up and down my shaft faster now, was a poor substitute, I realised. It got me to thinking... if her mouth felt that much better—really, exponentially better—than my hand... what would her cunt feel like? I groaned, my eyes opening back up to the picture of the girl who looked so much like my stepsister on the glossy magazine page, flipping it again to see her exposing her cunt with both hands. What would Dawn's cunt feel like when I slid into it?

I caught myself with a start. *When...* That was the thought. Not if, but when. God, I didn't want to admit it, but it was true—I wanted to fuck my stepsister. My cock was swollen and aching with my lust for her. I turned the page to my all-time favourite pic, the girl's arse up in the air, his cum sliding down her arsehole and cunt.

Seeing Dawn's writing there in the margin made me want her even more, and the girl in the picture paled in comparison. I closed my eyes and imagined my stepsister's cunt instead, imagined what it would be like to slide my thick, throbbing length into her wetness. I licked my palm and slid it over my shaft, making my thumb and finger tight like the opening to her cunt. It felt great, and I made my fist tighter, like I was slipping up into the slippery sleeve of her wetness. Oh, Christ, I wanted her.

I could hear her voice in my head, "Don't you want to fuck me?" My cock jerked in response, my hand pumping hard, now, picturing my stepsister's arse up in the air, watching my cock slide in and out of her. Would she let me come inside of her? I moaned, imagining spurting my cum deep into her cunt, and that did it. My cock began to spasm, spilling hot jets of creamy white fluid all over my hand.

And I still couldn't get the image of my stepsister out of my head, even when I was spent. I was thinking about her as I cleaned up and stashed the magazines. I was still thinking about her when I went into the house. She wasn't sleeping on the sofa anymore, and the shower was running upstairs. I decided I was going to have to get out of the house. Maybe getting a job as soon as possible wasn't such a bad idea after all.

I decided on cold pizza for lunch. Dawn came down, wearing her robe, her hair wet. She smiled at me as she passed by, sorting through the cupboards, but she turned away empty handed with a sigh, opening the fridge. I chewed my pizza, washing it down with a soda, watching her rummage through, looking for something.

"How are you feeling?" I swallowed down the last of my food.

"Better. Ta." She put some lettuce, tomatoes and cucumbers on the counter. "I think that Irn-Bru really works."

"Always does for me when I've gotten tanked up." I watched her cut lettuce and put it into a bowl. She licked her fingers after cutting the tomato. Bloody hell, my cock was knocking at my zipper, and I was just watching her holding a cucumber in her hand!

I sighed, taking my dishes to the sink and rinsing them. I felt her press in behind me, resting her cheek against my back. Her body was incredibly warm, her breasts soft against me as she slipped her arms around my waist.

"Davey…" She rubbed against me. "You're so good."

"I'm not." I swallowed hard as she slid her hands under my shirt, moving them over the bare skin of my belly, making me shiver. "I'm really, really not."

"You are." She moved her hand down over my jeans. I cringed, knowing she would find how hard I was. Part of me really wanted her to, and another part of me was embarrassed, still. Especially in the light of day. "Ohhh... yeah. Really, really good."

I groaned, her hand small and warm against my crotch, her breasts moving against my back as she rubbed me. She popped my button open with her other hand, unzipping my jeans. I let her. My cock wanted her, and the more she touched me, the more my head was starting to agree.

"Turn around," she whispered. I did, watching her pull my jeans down to my knees and kneel in front of me. She slipped my cock between her lips, looking up at me. My memory hadn't failed me. It was ten, a hundred times better than my hand.

I looked down at her. God, her eyes. She looked like she loved doing it, like it was the biggest turn-on in the world to have my cock sliding down her throat. That drove me wild. I grunted, thrusting deep into her mouth. She slid her nails up my thighs, grazing them over my balls. Oh, Christ, that was good! She cupped them in her hand, rolling them around. Gah! My knees felt like they were going to buckle.

"You like that little brother?" Her hand stroked my shaft. I nodded, looking at her through half-closed eyes. She reached down and opened her robe, shrugging it off her shoulders. It fell onto the linoleum in a pink, satiny puddle, exposing her body to my eyes.

Then she stood, pressing against me the whole way, her nipples grazing my thighs, my belly, her hand still wrapped around my cock. She stood on her tiptoes, putting her other hand behind my head and pulling my mouth to hers.

The kiss was long and slow, and she tasted like toothpaste. My tongue tried to draw hers further in, and my hands slid over her back, down the curve of her arse. My cock was pulsing against the soft flesh of her belly and she wiggled against it, making me moan into her mouth.

Without breaking the kiss, she took my hands and put them on her breasts. I still couldn't get over the fact that I was tweaking my stepsister's nipples, making her gasp and writhe and roll her hips. They were fat and grew fatter in my fingers as I tugged and pulled on them.

I reached my arms down and locked them behind her arse, lifting her up until her breasts were pressed against my face. I sucked at them, first one, then the other, rolling my tongue around the thick buds.

Dawn moaned and gripped my shoulders, her head going back. She wrapped her legs around my waist, and I held her there, now sucking her nipple hard, drawing it deep into my mouth.

She got heavy after a minute, so I turned toward the counter, propping her up on the edge. This freed my hands, and one went to the breast that my mouth wasn't covering, while the other quickly found its way between her open legs.

She groaned when I parted her lips with my fingers. She was soaking wet! My cock was pointed straight up, as if aiming for her. The thought kept returning, as hard as I tried to push it away. I wanted to get inside her.

"Put your fingers in me," she panted. I searched through the wet folds of flesh, looking for her centre. I wasn't fast enough, and Dawn guided me, showing me her opening. I slowly sank a finger into her. She was so smooth inside that it was actually shocking to me. How could anything be that soft?

"Two fingers." She rocked against my hand.

I slid another one in, moving my fingers at an easy pace, in and out of her cunt. It made a deliciously sloppy wet sound that had my cock swelling, like it was stretching higher, eager to do its part. The thought of making those sounds with my cock inside of her was too much. My head was just getting in the way, now, my thoughts racing, and I wanted to turn it off and let my body take over.

"Put three in." She leaned back on her elbows, putting her feet up in the counter and opening her knees. I could look down now and watch my fingers slipping in and out of her.

"More?" I watched my two fingers stretching her flesh. I pulled them out for a moment, her juices thick, clinging to my fingers in clear strands.

"Unless you want to put your cock in me?"

I met her eyes, and then looked down at her cunt again. Open, wet, waiting. All I had to do was slide inside. She wanted me to fuck her, I wanted to fuck her. Why wasn't I fucking her, then?

"Come on." She slid her arse to the edge of the counter and opened her lips with her fingers. "Put that hard cock in me. You know you want to."

Fuck yes, I wanted to! My cock most definitely wanted to be buried balls-deep inside of her—it was the voice in my head that was the problem. This was my stepsister! If we crossed that line, there was just no going back. Somehow I could rationalize everything up to that point, like some virgin girl who thought oral or anal sex wasn't "real sex." It was strange, but true.

"God, I have to have your cock!" She moaned, slipping two of her own fingers inside. "Please, Davey. Fuck me. Put it in me."

"Oh hell!" I groaned, taking my cock in my hand and aiming it for her. Her eyes were bright, and she grabbed me, sliding me up and down her wet slit. Oh Christ, that didn't just feel good—that was fucking incredible! She worked me up over her clit and back down, her eyes half-closed, her breath coming fast.

"You gonna fuck me, little brother?" She slipped the tip of my cock down toward her hole. I winced, grabbing her hips and pushing her back a little on the counter.

"Dawn, we can't." I gritted my teeth. My cock was wet with her juices and longing for more of her warmth.

"Oh, hell!" She swore, rolling her eyes and leaning back on her elbows. "Are you serious?"

I closed my eyes. I was off my trolley. I had to be. I had a willing, waiting, wet cunt in front of me, and I was saying no? I was definitely off my head. But my head was the problem. It kept screaming, "This is your *sister*!"

"You can't leave me like this," she pleaded. "David, I have to have your cock. Please!"

"I'll lick you," I said, a peace offering.

She sighed. "Noooo... Oh my God, I want you so much..."

I groaned, leaning over her and pressing my face against the flesh of her belly. She smelled clean, like soap. "Dawnie, I can't. I just can't." I looked up, pleading with my eyes. "You're my sister."

She frowned for a moment, and then her gaze left mine, moving over the counter beside her. She smiled, getting that mischievous Dawnie look in her eye again. I watched as she picked up the cucumber that she had put on the counter to cut up for her salad.

"Here." She handed it to me, grinning. "Then you can fuck me with this."

My eyes widened, but I took it. "With this?"

"If I can't have you, then this will have to do." She nodded, opening her legs wide.

I hesitated. It was far larger than my cock, thicker through the middle for sure. Could she take this inside of her? How? I found myself curious to see.

"Come on." She spread her lips open, showing me her cunt. "I want to be fucked."

There was no way! That tiny little hole, and she wanted me to slide this huge cucumber in there?

I pressed the tip to her flesh, and she shivered. "Cold," she murmured. "Go on." Further, another inch. I watched her lips spreading over it, taking it in. "Deeper. Come on, David."

I slid it steadily into her, watching in awe as her pink, wet flesh stretched as she took it into her, inch by inch.

When it was about halfway in, she squirmed. "No further than that...okay?" I nodded, my breath coming fast.

"Lick me."

I leaned in toward her, nosing her clit, finding it with my tongue. She moaned, wiggling, and ran a hand through my hair, guiding my head. "Yessssss, right there."

I licked at her, holding the cucumber, buried halfway in. She started rocking against me, whimpering. Her cunt tasted clean and sweet, and I swallowed her, wanting more.

"Now, fuck me!" She rolled her hips. I started moving the cucumber out of her and then back in, slow and easy, keeping my mouth fastened against her, my tongue teasing her clit.

"Faster," she begged, and I obeyed, moving it in and out of her more rapidly, the thick length of the vegetable opening her wide. "Oooohhh, yes, harder!"

I was shoving it in her now, my tongue making circles around and around her clit, catching a rhythm. She was fucking back, lifting her hips, rolling them, and I struggled to keep my tongue moving where I knew she wanted it.

"Ooooo! You fuck me so good!" she moaned. "Harder!"

So I did, as hard as I could, looking up at her, propped on her elbows and watching me fuck her with the cucumber, my tongue licking fast at her clit.

She looked at me through half-closed eyes and whispered, "Don't you wish it was your cock, baby brother?"

I groaned against her flesh at the cruel words, twisting the cucumber in her cunt and making her gasp. She seemed to like that, so I continued to twist it as I fucked her, back and forth, in and out.

"Ohhhh God, I wish it was you." She looked down at me. "I wish it was your big, hard cock fucking me like that."

Oh hell. Me, too, I thought, plunging it deeper still, ignoring what she'd said earlier about "no further." She didn't seem to care, she was breathing fast, and bucking against me, taking more and more of the dark green shaft into her cunt. I worked it hard and fast inside of her, my face coated in her juices, my cock a steel rod throbbing for release.

She started to make that sweet, telltale noise, "uh, uh, uh," and I moaned against her flesh, fucking her a little harder, licking faster still.

"Ohhhh you're so good, little brother," she whispered. "So fucking gooooooood!" She gasped and shuddered and grabbed my hair, pushing her hips up to meet me and shoving my mouth against her so hard that I couldn't breathe, and I didn't care. She was flooding my face with her sweetness, her cunt spasming around the cucumber again and again.

She collapsed on the counter, moaning still, and I looked down at the vegetable still half-submerged inside of her, slick and wet. I slid it out, slow, and she moaned, as if she didn't want to let it go. She breathed a sigh, reaching for me, and I helped her sit.

Smiling, she took the cucumber from me, licking at the tip, tasting herself on it.

"Want to see something?" There was that Dawnie look, so mischievous. I nodded, grabbing my cock as I watched her. It was begging for attention. I just couldn't help stroking it a little as her tongue ran over the phallic vegetable, licking it just like I remembered her licking my cock.

I groaned when she took it into her mouth, watching her lips stretch over the impossible girth of the thing, taking more and more, and more still! She worked it in, gagging a little, and that made my hand move even faster over my shaft, until it was two thirds of the way into her mouth. I stared, fascinated, and then she took it out, slow, meeting my eyes.

"Neat trick, huh?"

"Show me again," I said, my voice hoarse, squeezing the tip of my cock until it was red bordering on purple.

"I'm guessing you don't mean on this." She smiled, setting the cucumber on the counter, and sliding off it. "Come here."

She led me over to one of the kitchen chairs, sitting me down in it and pulling my jeans and boxers off. I leaned back a little, watching her. God, she was beautiful—I couldn't stop looking at her, the way her breasts swayed gently as she settled herself between my legs, the soft swell of her belly and thighs, the sweet way she tucked her hair behind her ears before she leaned in to give her full attention to my cock.

I knew I wasn't going to last long, but I wanted it to. I wanted to sit in this chair and watch her forever. I couldn't believe I was doing this, letting her do this, and yet I had never wanted anything more.

"You want me to suck your cock, baby brother?" She ran her hands up my thighs. I just nodded. "Then say it."

"I want you to suck my cock," I gasped, watching as she kissed the tip, teasing it and flicking it with her tongue.

"'I want you to suck my cock... big sister,'" she whispered, then licked up the throbbing vein underneath my shaft, from base to tip. "Say it."

I groaned, wiggling in the chair. She was killing me. "Dawn, please."

"Say it." She sat back, putting her hands on her knees, waiting. She licked her lips, staring at my cock, and then met my eyes and smiled. "Tell your big sister you want her to suck you until you come."

The words were caught in my throat. Saying them out loud felt like an admission. I struggled, watching as she rubbed her hands over her breasts. "Don't you want to come all over my tits, little brother?"

"Please!" Oh, hell! I felt like I was going to burst if I didn't have her. I swallowed hard. "Please, big sister... suck my cock."

She grinned, leaning into me and taking my shaft in her hand. "See?" She licked all around the tip. I groaned. "That wasn't so hard, was it?"

I shook my head, watching my shaft disappearing into her mouth. I tried to keep my eyes open, so I could remember every delicious moment, but it was difficult. Every time her mouth sank down on me, my eyes wanted to roll back into my head. She was all mouth, up and down my shaft, taking me deep, moving agonizingly slow, like she wanted to make it last, too.

My hands moved to her hair, still damp from the shower, guiding her head. I couldn't help pressing her down a little. God, I loved the sound of her gagging on it! She curled her tongue underneath my shaft as she slid her mouth down, and then rolled it slowly around the tip as she came up. My legs were shaking, and I was trying hard not to come. I didn't want it to end.

"I want your cum." She kissed all around the tip, her eyes never leaving mine. "Tell me when you're close. I want you to shoot it all over my tits."

I groaned, grabbing her hair and shoving her back down on my cock. She squealed a little, and then went fast to work, using her mouth to squeeze and suck me until I thought I was going to die. I could feel my balls tightening and I bucked hard against her, deep into her throat. I was torn, wanting to shoot my cum into her mouth, and wanting to see it splashed all over my stepsister's gorgeous tits.

"Dawn," I warned, the sensation beginning to edge toward the peak. She worked even harder, then, moaning and sucking and twisting her mouth over my shaft. Oh fuck, that was too much, I couldn't hold it any more. I started to come, shooting the first blast into her mouth, and she swallowed it, looking up at me.

She grabbed me, pointing me toward her chest, and I thrust into her pumping hand, growling and moaning, shooting hot streams of cum onto her waiting tits. She moaned, too, rubbing my cock through the wetness, spreading my cum over her nipples. She continued to stroke me, milking me, squeezing every drop out.

"God," I groaned, throwing my head back. "We are so bad."

"Good!" She kissed the tip of my softening cock. I looked down at her, covered in my cum—and I thought she couldn't look any more beautiful before? Boy, I was wrong.

I'd never seen anything more beautiful than she was in that moment.

"I think I'm gonna need another shower." She smiled, standing up and walking over to retrieve her robe. I watched her put it on, pulling her hair out from underneath it, a sweet, feminine gesture. I pulled my boxers and jeans back up, tucking and buttoning and zipping quickly. For some reason, I didn't want her to see me, now.

"I gotta make phone calls." I had forgotten that I left my paper outside. When I went out to get it, it had blown all over the yard, and I spent ten minutes picking it all back up again.

When I went back into the house, I could hear Dawn up in her room, playing the radio. She was singing. I stood for a long time at the bottom of the stairs, cooling my hot forehead against the wall. Instead of going up, I slipped on my shoes and went outside for a walk.

* * * *

"Steak and kidney pie again?" Dawn complained, slipping into the chair next to me.

"You're home all day this week." Mum gave her a quelling look. "You can always cook, if you want something different."

"I like pie." I spooned some onto my plate. Mum smiled at me, but Dawn stuck out her tongue and pinched my leg.

"Your Mum has the best pie." Dad winked over at her. She blushed, and I glanced over at my stepsister, as if to say, 'Did I hear that right?'

"Ew!" Dawn reached for the salad. "Get a room."

"We have one." My father poured himself some milk. "It's upstairs. I pay for it. Speaking of which—how's the job hunting, David?"

Inwardly, I groaned, but mumbled, "Fine," and shovelled some potatoes into my mouth.

"Salad, David?" Mum handed me the bowl when Dawn was done. I reached for it, and then I saw them. Cucumbers. Panicked, I looked at my stepsister. It couldn't possibly be!

She grinned at me and bit into one, crunching noisily. "These are the best cucumbers, Mum."

"They've had such good ones at the market, lately," Mum said, and I watched, horrified, as she tasted one. "Nice and big."

"Mmmm!" Dawn grinned, nudging me under the table. "I know!"

Chapter Five

"David!"

Oh bugger. Mum again. I buried my head under my pillow and pretended for the third time that I hadn't heard her. Couldn't a bloke sleep in on a Saturday?

I used to live for the weekends. Now they had turned into endless days of chores that Mum found needed doing around the house, and of course Dad seemed to be in agreement— he said I needed to keep busy, since I wasn't at school anymore.

"David!"

Oh hell. It was Dad this time. She had called in the big guns. I threw the pillow off my head and grabbed a pair of jeans from next to my bed, tugging them on. He opened my door without knocking just as I was pulling on a t-shirt. "Oh, good, glad you're up."

"Yeah." I sighed, running a hand through my hair and waiting. I knew it was coming.

"I've got to fix your mother's planters," Dad said. "Get some breakfast and come out back to help me, would you?"

"Okay." I gave him a little salute as he shut the door. Damn. Doing chores for Mum was better than spending the day handing tools over to Dad—listening to him swear at whatever piece or part wouldn't fit into the correct spot and then taking it out on me just because I handed him the wrong spanner or whatever.

All that meant that when I stormed into the kitchen, I was in a fairly black mood. Mum was washing up the breakfast dishes, and I grabbed a bowl and a box of Frosties, standing at the window and shoveling in bites while I watched Dad pulling Mum's planters out. Dawn was lying in the sunlounger watching him, wearing her white bikini and soaking up the near-afternoon sun.

"So what's wrong with the ones you have?" I asked through a mouth full, glancing over at Mum. "They look fine to me."

"They're rotting in the back." She reached over me for a tea towel. "Your father said he didn't use the treated wood, but he's got some in the shed he's going to replace it with."

I stared at her for a moment, milk dribbling down my chin as I turned back to look out the window. Dad was heading for the shed, now—to get the wood for the planter, I assumed. The very wood that my porn collection was hidden under! Fuck! I threw my bowl in the sink, still half-full, and bolted for the back door.

"David!" Mum called after me, sounding disgusted. "You didn't even finish—"

I didn't hear the rest. I burst out of the door in my bare feet, jumping down the steps and landing in front of Dad just as he was about to open the shed door. He took a step back when I barrelled out in front of him, and stood staring at me with his mouth open.

"Hey!" I slapped him on the shoulder. "Here I am! Reporting for duty! What can I do? Can I get something for you out of the shed?"

Dawn sat half-up, lowering her sunglasses to look at us. I glanced over his shoulder at her, pleading her with my eyes.

"Actually, you can go down to the basement and get my toolbox." Dad moved to step around me. I matched his movement, still blocking the way.

"That wood is kind of heavy, Dad." I looked over at Dawn for some help. "Let me carry it for you. Dawn can go get your tool box."

"I will not!" She snorted, leaning back and sliding her sunglasses up.

"Come on, David." Dad stepped around me and grabbed the shed door. "Go on and get my toolbox."

I widened my eyes at Dawn and she shrugged but was silently laughing. Some help she was! I bounded up the back steps, pulling open the door and running through the kitchen, nearly knocking Mum over on my way toward the basement.

"David!" she cried, sounding exasperated, but I didn't stop. I flew down the stairs and turned the corner toward Dad's work room. His toolbox was under the work bench, and I leaned under to grab it, hitting my head on the table as I came up.

"Fuck!" I swore, rubbing my head as I lugged the toolbox back up the stairs, slowed down now by the weight.

"Everything all right?" Mum asked as she opened the back door for me.

"Ta," I panted, answering cryptically: "I'll know in a minute."

Dawn sat up again as I came back out, still wearing a crooked smile. Dad was still in the shed. I set the toolbox down and peered inside the shed door. He was fishing through the boards, whistling something. It didn't sound or look like he'd found anything—yet. I let out a sigh of relief.

"Hey, Dad," I called in. "I have your toolbox. Want me to carry any of that?"

Dad looked up from where he was kneeling. From the angle I was watching from, I could actually see the corner of one of my porn mags resting under the boards just on the other side of his knee. The sight of it so close to discovery made me feel dizzy and ill.

"You're awfully helpful today." Dad stood and brushed his hands off. "Here, take these four outside." He pointed to the boards he had laid aside. I grabbed them and propped them over my shoulder, carrying them out of the shed.

"Come on, Dad." I set the boards on the ground between his toolbox and the planter. "Let's get this project started!"

Dawn was silently laughing, her belly and breasts shaking as she covered her mouth so Dad wouldn't hear her. I gave her the finger and she made a wanking motion between her legs, sticking her tongue out at me.

I'd been so panicked about the possibility of Dad finding my porn collection that I'd barely noticed her in her white bikini, but now the motion of her hand between her legs drew my eyes there and I found myself staring.

"All right, Davey." Dad slapped me on the shoulder as he came out. "Let's get to work!"

At that point, I was just thankful that no one was poking around the shed anymore and I was pretty much willing to do anything. Dawn laid back down to soak up some sun, and Dad and I got to work, pulling apart the old planter.

Mum hadn't planted anything in it this year, because the wood had rotted, so we didn't have to worry about that. The wood had split in several places, though, making it harder to pull apart. I was using the claw end of the hammer at one end, and Dad was at the other, trying to pry the nails up.

"Next time," I grunted, wiping sweat off my brow with the tail end of my t-shirt. "Don't use such long-arse nails!"

Dad yanked a nail free and it tinkled on the cement. "Come on." He started on another one, grunting with the effort. "Don't be a nancy boy. Just give it some welly!"

"Yeah!" Dawn called, dropping her sunglasses and looking at me. She had that Dawnie-grin on. "Give it some welly, David!"

"Nosey Parker!" I made a face at her and grabbed my hammer, starting to work on the board again. By the time we got the back taken off, I was sweating like mad, and I pulled off my t-shirt. Dawn whistled and I threw her a dirty look.

"Come on, go starkers." She grinned. "No one can see."

"Good thing." I tossed my t-shirt at her. It landed shy of her chair. "You might as well be, in that thing."

Dad glanced over at her, frowning. "The boy has a point."

"Oh, naff off, both of you!" Dawn turned over on her belly on the lounge chair. Her bikini bottoms pulled across her arse, and I could actually see the outline of her lips in them. She swung her feet, not looking at us, her body glistening with oil. I noticed that she was actually getting a little more brown.

"Don't get cheeky, Miss." Dad tossed aside the old boards and headed toward the shed.

"Whoa! Ho!" I grabbed his arm. "Hey, Dad, where are you going?"

He looked down at my hand on his arm and back up at me, his eyebrows raised. "I need my saw," he said slowly, taking my hand off his arm. "Are you all right?"

I nodded, my eyes shifting to the shed. "Fine."

"You're a bit wonky today." He frowned, setting off toward the shed.

My jaw was clenching and unclenching as I sat on one of the patio chairs, waiting for him as he rummaged around in there.

"What's the matter, little brother?" Dawn smiled over at me. "Afraid you're going to get caught?"

I glanced over at her and saw that she had turned onto her back and was tracing the outline of her nipples through her bikini top. They were hard and poking through the material. My eyes nearly popped out of my head.

"Dawn!" I hissed, glancing toward the shed. I could still hear Dad sorting through things in there. I was just praying he didn't go near the boards again.

"What?" She pinched her nipples through the material, making them even harder, and I could feel my cock responding, remembering how they felt in my mouth, how they looked when she was sitting up on the counter, letting me fuck her with the cucumber. Holy hell.

"Fancy these?" She lifted her breasts, rubbing her hands over the material. She slipped one hand under the white cloth, from the top, and I could see her working her hand over her bare skin.

I watched, transfixed. She pulled her bikini top down over her breasts completely then, shaking her shoulders, making her breasts sway. I stared, my cock an iron rod in my jeans now, my breath caught in my throat.

"Dawn," I gulped, glancing toward the shed and realizing I couldn't hear Dad anymore. She smiled, pulling her top back up and stretching her arms over her head with a fake yawn as Dad came out of the shed carrying a saw.

"Damned thing was hiding," he mumbled, calling over to me. "Come hold this steady, David!"

"Coming..." My voice was faint as I stood. She was staring at my crotch and I flushed, knowing my erection must be clearly outlined.

I went over to help Dad, but I couldn't help looking over at my stepsister. She was watching us, lying back on her elbows, her feet pressed together, her legs open. The outline of her pussy under the material was making me loopy. It was all I could think about.

Dad was sawing a board that he'd put up onto a breeze block, and I was supposed to be holding it steady. His back was to my stepsister, but I was facing her, and had a clear view of her full body, lying there glistening in the sun. She saw me watching her and grinned, and I inwardly groaned, but I couldn't look away as she started teasing her nipples again.

Dad sawed through that board and began measuring another, his back still to my stepsister. She continued to tease me, pinching and pulling her nipples through the material, making a little "o" with her mouth.

"Hold this." Dad put another board up. I put my knee on it, my eyes on my stepsister's body. She was rubbing her hands over her belly, sliding them lower and lower. I licked my lips as I watched, my cock throbbing in my jeans now.

Dad was sawing away, grunting and wiping sweat from his brow. The sensation made me think of fucking, and I couldn't help but think of fucking my stepsister. I had the brief fantasy of just pulling her bikini bottoms aside and plunging my cock into her right there on the lounge chair— that's how much I wanted her.

Dawn slipped her fingers under the top elastic band of the bikini bottoms and I watched, wide-eyed, as she began to play with herself. I could see her hand working underneath the material, and I remembered exactly what she felt like inside, how soft and smooth and warm.

She saw me watching her and grinned, pulling the material aside with one finger and showing me her cunt. I glanced down at Dad, who was still sawing away, and then back to my stepsister, exposing herself to me. She was the most beautiful thing I'd ever seen, lying there with her cunt spread open, sliding her fingers up and down her slit.

When she started fingering herself, I lost it. I think I was unconsciously leaning forward, to get a better view, because my knee slipped off the board and it went flying up, nearly hitting me in the bollocks.

"Flippin' 'eck!" Dad looked at me with a frown. "David, will you concentrate?"

"Sorry." I glanced back at Dawn, who had stopped playing, but was now licking her fingers. Oh God. I could almost taste her pussy. She grinned at me and blew a kiss. My whole body felt flushed and I was grateful that it was hot out.

I tried to keep my mind off my stepsister and just pay attention to helping Dad. We got the rest of the boards cut, and Dawn rolled over onto her belly and thankfully appeared to fall asleep. Her sunglasses were askew, and she was drooling onto the towel underneath her, her hand trailing down onto the patio. Her bikini bottoms were riding up her sweet, rounded arse, and I wanted to touch her so badly it almost hurt.

I grabbed a hammer and started pounding along with Dad, helping him nail the boards along the back of the planter. I pounded as hard as I could, hoping if I expended enough energy, I might eliminate the throbbing ache between my legs.

It actually seemed to have the opposite effect, especially when my stepsister rolled onto her back again, throwing her arm over her eyes and giving me a clear view of her rising and falling breasts, the material pulled taut over them.

"Ta, for all your help, David," Dad said as I was pounding in the last nail on my side and he was putting tools away in the toolbox.

"Nothing like two big, strong, sweaty men working on a project." Dawn shaded her eyes as she looked over at us. She was grinning.

"Cheeky." Dad smiled fondly at her. Jesus. If he had any idea! My mouth went dry at the thought.

"I'm going to need a shower." I stood and arched my back. It hurt from being bent over so long. "Mind if I go, Dad?"

"Go ahead." He was closing up the shed. I was pretty sure my porn collection was safe from prying eyes, but I was clearly going to have to find a new hiding spot.

Dawn smiled at me as I passed, nudging me with her toe, but I ignored her. I was going to go jerk off in the shower and come all over the wall as I imagined fucking her so hard she screamed—but I wasn't going to let on.

I ran the water in the shower, stripping as I waited for it to get hot. My cock was still hard—it felt like I had been hard for hours. The thought of Dawn's exposed pussy, her teasing smile and that little "o" of her mouth, had my erection aiming skyward the minute it was free from my boxers.

I stood holding it in my hand, squeezing it, trying to appease it a little and ease the ache as I adjusted the water temperature. The hot water felt incredible and I stood there for a minute, just getting wet. Every time I closed my eyes, I could see my stepsister's cunt, her thick lips and pink centre.

I washed my hair, but my hand seemed to have a mind of its own as it snaked down to my cock, pumping it gently as I remembered how she looked as she fingered herself. Jesus, but she was hot. What would it feel like to fuck her, I wondered? What would it feel like to slip my prick between those fat lips and sink deep inside of her? My hand moved faster at the thought.

"David?" The knock on the door made me jump. It was Dawn! "I have to pee!"

Oh Christ. We only had one washroom. "Okay," I called. She opened the door and came in. The shower curtain was pulled tight, but I could hear her peeing, and the sound was strangely erotic. My hand moved even faster.

"Don't flush!" I reminded her. If she did, I'd be standing under a well-needed cold shower.

"I won't." She peeked around the curtain.

"Hey!" I jumped, my hand moving immediately away from my erection.

I flicked water at her and she grinned, pulling the curtain aside and stepping in, completely nude. She looked down at my cock, which hadn't flagged in the least. I stared at her in shock, but she nuzzled up to me, sucking at the skin of my neck and pressing her sun-warmed, oily body against mine.

"You know you want to." She hooked her leg around mine and ground her cunt against me. My cock was trapped, pressed into her belly.

"Mum and Dad," I whispered, groaning when her hand squeezed my cock.

"They're in the kitchen, eating." She tugged gently between my legs, rubbing the tip of me all over her oily belly. "Don't you want to have something, too?"

She took my hand and pressed it over her mound. Her lips were full and swollen, hot to the touch, even under the water. She leaned against the back wall of the shower, putting her leg up and spreading her lips.

"Eat it." She showed me with her fingers. I went down on my knees like a starving man, the water of the shower hot against my back as I dove into her pussy, licking and sucking with all the lust I'd been holding in over the past few hours. I forgot about everything—I forgot she was my stepsister, I forgot my parents might catch us, I forgot how incredibly wrong it all was. The smell and feel and taste of her made me forget, and I drowned myself in her juices, licking and swallowing her like I couldn't get enough.

"Oh hell!" She rocked her hips against my mouth, her fingers tugging at her nipples. "That's it. You're so good, baby brother. Lick my cunt!"

The sound of the words made me crazy, and I grabbed her hips, wiggling my tongue and face against her snatch, faster and faster. She moaned, grabbing my wet hair and grinding against my face, just using my tongue now to get herself off. It was so hot that I thought I might come right there—my cock was throbbing for release. That was when she started making those little Dawnie "uh-uh-uh's" and I thought I would just die.

"I'm gonna come all over your face!" She arched her back and came in my mouth, her body shaking and quivering. She nearly collapsed, but I caught her, standing and holding her body against me, the water rushing around us both. She was biting and kissing my shoulder and upper arm, still gasping and shivering.

"Oooooo God…"She looked up at me, with a half-smile and half-closed eyes, her wet hair turning dark. "I can't get enough of you."

"I know how you feel." I leaned in and kissed her mouth. She met my kiss, wrapping her arms around my neck and tugging at the back of my hair. She reached around me for the soap and the flannel, starting to wash me up, running her hands all over my body. It felt incredible, and I watched her, seeing her eyes following her hands, over my chest, my belly, down to my cock.

She was all business between my legs, washing and scrubbing, but refusing to spend too much time. I was still hard as hard as a rock. She made me turn around and then she scrubbed my back, her little fingers slipping between the crack of my arse, making me jump.

"My turn," I said, taking the flannel from her and starting to wash her. She moaned when I rubbed the cloth over her breasts, tweaking her nipples with my fingers. I washed under them, lifting them in my hands, feeling their incredible weight.

Her belly was soft and rounded, and turning brown. Her breasts were pale in comparison now, showing the triangle of her bikini lines. I washed between her legs, pinning her to the wall with my body and rubbing the flannel there, over and over, watching her eyes flutter closed, her tongue moving to touch the corner of her mouth as she rocked against my hand.

"You're beautiful," I whispered into her ear, turning her around and washing the sloping curve of her back, the rise of her hips, the sweet globes of her arse. I slid my fingers in there, too, and she moaned and opened her legs when I did. That surprised me, and I touched her there for a moment, her little arsehole puckered and tight.

"I like that," she murmured over her shoulder, and it made me smile.

She let me wash her hair, and we both rinsed off under the water, which was beginning to turn from hot to lukewarm. I thought we'd been in here a long time—too long. I was starting to get nervous.

I turned off the water and pulled the shower curtain open, grabbing the towel, and rubbing her down with it. I only had one, but I used it damp on myself, drying what I could. My cock wouldn't give me a break, and it was pointing directly at her as she sat on the loo, smiling at me.

"Come here." She crooked her finger. I'd been hard so long it almost hurt, but her hand was like silk as she began stroking me. I groaned when she took the head into her mouth, running her tongue around and around.

"You have such a nice cock." She kissed the tip, looking up at me, her eyes, God, her eyes! When she looked at me like that, I felt like I wanted to give her anything, everything.

"I want it." She rubbed her thumb over the head, making me shudder with pleasure. "I want you to pound my pussy until I come all over your cock, little brother."

I groaned, feeling her tongue again, looking down to watch her suck me. Her eyes never left mine, and they were pleading, begging me, I could feel it in every motion, every look, every breath. I pushed my hips forward, sliding myself deeper into her mouth, imagining how sweet her pussy would feel wrapped around me.

"Come on." She stood and slid herself up on the washroom counter and opening her legs. I loved looking at her like that, open and ready, her eyes full of lust. "Put it in me."

"Dawn!" I shook my head. "We can't."

"Yes." She reached out and grabbed my cock. "Yes, we can. It's easy." She slipped the head of my prick up and down her slit. She was wet and slick. She aimed me at her hole, wiggling.

"See? Just push in." She rolled her hips. I could feel her pussy lips working around the head of my cock. Why did it seem like such a huge distance between this, and sliding in until I was buried inside of her? It seemed impossible.

"It feels soooo good, baby brother," she encouraged. "Don't you want to know what my cunt feels like?"

I took a shuddering breath, shaking my head. "I can't."

She sighed, her mouth turning to a little pout and my heart ached. "I want your cock," she begged, and she sounded like she was in as much pain as I was feeling. "Oh God, please?"

I shook my head, closing my eyes, and I felt her hand on me again and jumped. She was stroking me against her pussy, rubbing me up and down.

"This isn't fucking." She stroked me harder now, right against her clit. I nodded, watching her pussy lips moving as she tugged on my shaft. Dawn was rolling her hips, whimpering. She looked around and then reached over, grabbing one of the candles that Mum used when she took a bath. It was thick and long.

Dawn turned it upside down, so the wick end was pointing toward me. "Fuck me." She handed it to me. I didn't hesitate this time. I slid it between her lips and up into her pussy. She moaned, arching her back and pressing against me.

"That's it." She raised her legs, putting them up over my shoulders. I looked down, watching the candle disappearing into her flesh as I pushed it in and out of her. She was biting her lip, her eyes closed.

"Oh David!" She grabbed my cock and tugged on it. She rubbed it against her clit again, stroking it there as I worked the candle in and out of her cunt.

Her little hand was pumping hard, and the feel of her wet lips, the hard bud of her clit, was almost too much. I thrust into her hand, moving the candle deeper into her, twisting it, loving the sweet, wet, squelching noises it made as I fucked her.

"Dawnie," I groaned, feeling my orgasm fast approaching as she squeezed and rubbed me over her wet cunt. She was panting, meeting my thrusts, and I could almost imagine being shoved up inside her, fucking her hard like this, rocking toward heaven.

"I want you to come all over me," she whispered, her voice low with lust. "Shoot it all over my cunt, little brother."

I hissed as she rammed my cock hard up against her clit, pulling and tugging fast and furious now, and I shuddered, biting my lip to keep from crying out as jets of thick, hot fluid erupted from the tip of my cock, coating her clit and slipping down her slit toward the candle that I was still fucking her with.

"Uh-uh-uh!" Her voice was barely above a whisper, and I could feel the candle moving by itself in my hand as she came, like her pussy was trying to suck it deeper and deeper inside of her. She lay there for a moment, her whole body quivering, and I couldn't remember ever seeing anything more beautiful in my life.

She sat up with a smile and a sigh, wrapping her arms around me and kissing me on the mouth. I heard the candle slip out of her with a little "plop" and it fell to the floor between our legs.

"David?" We both jumped when the knock sounded and Mum's voice wafted through the door. We looked at each other with wide eyes.

"Yeah?"

"Hurry up, your Dad wants a shower, too," Mum said.

Dawn's hand was over her mouth, but her eyes were bright, like she was smiling under there.

"Okay, almost done!" I called. I grabbed the towel and wiped my cum off my stepsister's pussy, working it between her legs, making her squirm.

"That was close," I whispered as she hugged me.

"Not close enough," she whispered back, working her hips against mine and I groaned. I knew what she wanted, and God help me, I wanted it, too.

I couldn't seem to think about anything else, and while things were getting more and more out of hand, I still had a feeling she was going to get her way this summer, one way or another.

I just didn't think I could hold out much longer.

Chapter Six

I came into the house around mid-afternoon, pulling off my tie and throwing my suit jacket over a chair in the living room. I found myself calling for Dawn, but there was no answer. The house was quiet. I went into the kitchen, getting a glass of water at the sink, half-expecting to see her lying out in the garden in the lounge chair, but she wasn't there, either.

I'd spent the morning waiting in a queue of people for an interview at an insurance office. It was the only interview I had managed to get, and I was pretty sure I'd cocked it up completely. Just remembering it made me flush, and the thought of having to relate it all at the dinner table was really disheartening.

I considered turning on the telly for a while, but was too knackered and figured I'd just fall asleep on the sofa, so I just went upstairs. I took my suit pants and shirt off, hanging them over my doorknob for safekeeping, and then I climbed into bed in my boxers, not even bothering to crawl under the duvet. I hugged my pillow and drifted off.

I don't know how long I slept, but I was dreaming about my stepsister doing a headstand. When we were younger, she used to do headstands against the wall. She would practice for hours at a time, her face turning practically purple from being upside down for so long.

In my dream, she was wearing a skirt and no knickers, and she kept opening her legs wide and closing them again, grinning at me. Mum and Dad were sitting right there watching the telly, and I was watching her from between them on the sofa, my cock as hard as a rock watching her pussy spreading every time she opened her legs. I couldn't believe they weren't telling her to stop, but I couldn't keep myself from watching, either.

Then she collapsed on the floor and started crying, but Mum and Dad still didn't notice. I went over to her and was trying to comfort her, but she wouldn't stop crying. I don't know when I realised that the crying wasn't in my dream anymore.

The light had changed in the room, so I knew I'd been sleeping a while, but I could still hear my stepsister crying somewhere in the house.

"Dawn?" I called, still foggy, rolling over onto my back and looking toward my open door. No answer, but the crying continued. I stumbled out of bed, realizing that she was in her room. "Dawnie?"

I found her face down on her bed, wearing dungarees, still in her trainers, sobbing into her pillow. I sat next to her, putting my hand on her hair, which was in plaits.

"What is it?" I rubbed her shoulder.

"It's Ken!" Her voice was muffled, and then she turned her face to the side, giving a deep, hitching sigh. "Laurie and I went to the pictures this afternoon and we saw him there. He... he..."

"Don't tell me." I shook my head with a frown. "He was there with some slag?"

She turned over, crossing her arms over her chest. "How did you know?"

"Because, love." I wiped at her tears with my thumb. "Kenny Moore has the I.Q. of lint."

She smiled through her tears. "Shut up."

"It's true. Who was it?" I nudged her over and stretched out, leaning on my elbow next to her.

"Penny Thompson." She sniffed and made a face.

"Ah, see." I smiled, putting my other arm around her middle and pulling her belly to mine. "Now that proves it."

"What?" She wiped at her face with her hands, getting rid of the evidence.

"If he's choosing Penny over you?" I rolled my eyes. "Then I know he's an idiot. Besides, if sex was fast food, Penny'd have an arch over her head."

She laughed, and the sound was like music. It made me warm all over to see her smiling.

"What film did you see?"

"*Pride and Prejudice.*"

I made a face. "Could you have picked a bigger chick flick? There's no way Kenny Moore was at the cinema to see *Pride and Prejudice*. He can't even spell it."

She smiled. "No. I think they were seeing something else." She frowned then and I saw tears in her eyes again. "I don't think they were seeing much of anything, really, the way they were snogging in the lobby."

"Hey." I turned her face toward mine. I recognized the burning feeling in my chest. It was jealousy. The thought of my stepsister being with some other guy was actually making me jealous, now. *I'm doomed. I'm bloody well doomed.*

She looked up at me, and the emotion in her eyes made me melt. My dream had reminded me of when we were kids, and in her dungarees, with her hair in plaits, she looked almost like she used to when she would hold my hand and walk me to the corner shop and buy me sweets even though Mum told her not to.

"Do you know how beautiful you are?" I leaned in to kiss her. She made a little noise in her throat, kissing me back, her mouth soft. She even tasted like sweets—she must have been eating some at the cinema, because her lips were still sticky with it.

Her hand slipped behind my head and she pulled me in, her tongue finding mine, probing between my lips, darting in and out of my mouth. She tasted even sweeter now, a little like peppermint, and I sucked on her tongue, wanting more. Her leg found its way around mine, the heel of her trainer digging into my thigh, making me wince.

She seemed to sense my discomfort, and toed off her shoes, pulling me over onto her, hugging me between her thighs as we kissed. The fasteners on the front of her dungarees were digging into my chest and I fumbled with them, tossing the straps over her shoulders and pulling down the front over her black t-shirt. She may have been dressed like when we were kids, but the full, firm breasts with their hard nipples under my hand weren't a little girl's, and I could feel my erection growing against the thick seam between her legs.

"Would you like them off me?" she whispered in my ear, licking my neck and making me shiver as she slid her hands up and down my bare back, her nails raking lightly.

"Yes." I looked down at her. She was smiling again and her eyes bright, but no longer with tears.

She pushed me over onto my side and slid out from under me, letting her dungarees fall to her hips as she stood. Turning her back to me, she looked over her shoulder as she wiggled them over her bum. If someone had told me a week ago that I would be lying on my stepsister's bed, rubbing my cock through my boxers as I watched her strip, I would have told them they were crackers.

But here I was—and I couldn't take my eyes off her. Her knickers were white cotton and there was a little lace along the edge of the elastic around the legs. My eyes followed it around the curve and up between her thighs, where the gusset of her knickers was tucked between her lips. I could clearly see the indentation there when she bent over and stepped out of her dungarees.

She turned to me, still wearing her knickers and t-shirt and white ankle socks, her hair in plaits making her look more my age than hers. She even had sparkly little hair slides on either side, pulling her fringe back. The juxtaposition of her full, woman's body and the little girl accessories was darkly exciting to me, and I slipped my hand under my boxers to squeeze my aching cock.

"Do you really want me?" She stepped a little closer to the bed, close enough that I touched her thigh just to feel the satiny smoothness of it under my fingers. I couldn't believe she didn't know how incredible she was, how much I wanted her, how much any man in his right mind would want her! My stepsister was the sexiest woman I'd ever seen, and I struggled with how to tell her that.

"I want to fuck you." I slid my hand up her inner thigh and massaging her pussy through her knickers. Her eyes widened and she moaned, rocking against my fingers.

"Do you mean it?" she whispered, and I realised I did. I couldn't deny it anymore. She was the hottest, sweetest, most delicious woman I'd ever met, and I wanted her more than I'd ever wanted anything before. I thought about her, dreamed about her, fantasized about her—hell, I loved her. I'd loved her my whole life.

"Yes." I nodded, watching her peel her t-shirt off over her head, revealing a shiny, lace-edged black bra underneath that made me gasp. It was such a shock, to see something so sexy paired with her innocent looking white cotton knickers, and it made my cock jump in my hand.

She leaned over and kissed my belly, her tongue making lazy circles as she crawled back onto the bed in her bra and knickers. Her mouth kissed its way down from my navel, following the line of dark hair that disappeared from sight. Her breath was warm as she worked her way toward my cock, inching my boxers down as she went.

I let her take over down there and pulled her arse close to me, running my hands over it through her knickers, cupping her mound, just feeling the heat of her. She made a little noise when I did, wiggling back against me, arching, and I groaned when her hand wrapped around my shaft, squeezing it and tugging.

She lifted her leg, positioning herself over me and inching back. I could smell her already, even through her knickers. She had me in her mouth now, working her tongue and lips up and down my cock, moaning and making wet sucking noises. The sound of her alone was making me batty, and the sensation was far beyond.

"Lick me," she murmured as her mouth came up on my cock. I slipped my hand under the elastic of her knickers but she moved her hips, edging away.

"Through my knickers." She opened her legs wider and wiggled toward my mouth. I groaned, wrapping my arms around her hips and pulling her in to me. I could smell her strong now, with my nose buried in the gusset, and I realised that it retained her scent. The heat of her was incredible, even through the material.

I licked at the soft cloth, making it wetter and wetter with my tongue, trying to find her clit through the layers. Her moan of pleasure told me I'd found the right place and I moved my mouth over it again and again until her knickers were soaked and I couldn't tell whether it was from my saliva or her juices.

She had all but forgotten about my cock, which stood throbbing straight up in her hand. I could feel her breath against my thigh, my belly, my balls, as she rocked on me and moaned. She slipped her hand between her legs, tucking her knickers deeper into her slit, into the crack of her arse.

"Here." She pressed her index finger against the material, showing me. "Lick me here."

I followed her direction, finding the place with my tongue, realizing after a moment that I was licking her little arsehole! I could feel it, puckered and tight under my tongue through the cloth as it got wetter and wetter. She squirmed and moaned and seemed to really like it, so I licked faster, probing it with my tongue, making her gasp.

"Yesssss!" She put her hand over her knickers and rubbed as I continued to lick her arse. "Oh fuck, David, yes!"

I could feel her body tightening, her belly quivering, and I knew she was close. Her fingers were rubbing her knickers all over her pussy, back and forth, 'round and 'round, and I could hear how wet she was.

I grabbed her hips, shoving my tongue into her arse through her knickers as deep as I could, wiggling my tongue, probing hard. She came then, shuddering and crying out louder than I'd ever heard her, nearly screaming, panting and thrashing on top of me like some wild thing. I had to hold her tight to keep her from bucking right off, and she shivered against me as I continued to lick and suck at the gusset of her knickers.

She collapsed onto me, panting, her hand squeezing my cock so hard I thought it must have turned purple. It took her a moment, but she sat up on me, still gasping, turning around and straddling my chest. She had a lazy, Cheshire cat smile on, and that, along with the feel of her cunt through her knickers against my skin, her wetness and heat, made me dizzy with lust.

She stroked my cheek, her eyes bright. "You are so fucking good, baby brother," she murmured, running a hand through my hair. I loved and hated it when she reminded me like that. There were moments I could almost forget that she was my big sister, but then she would say something like that and bring it rushing forward again. It was so wrong, but it felt too good to stop. I couldn't be strong anymore—I wanted her too much.

I reached up and cupped her breasts in my hands through her bra. She arched her back a little, her hips rocking as she did, moving her wetness over my belly and chest. Her nipples were hard, and I wanted them. I wanted to see them, suck them, feel them get fat and swollen in my mouth. I struggled with the hook at the front of her bra and she pushed my hand away, undoing it with a smile.

I watched in awe as her breasts tumbled out with a sweet, gentle bounce, her dark pink nipples settling to point to the wall behind my head. I reached for them, grasping them both in my hands and rubbing them together, flicking my thumbs over her nipples. She moaned when I did that, and I wrapped my arms around her back, pulling her in to me and sucking her nipple into my mouth.

It grew swollen as I worked it with my tongue, sucking hard, while I tugged the other one in my fingers, making her shiver. She pressed her hands against the wall behind my head, trying to steady herself as her hips rocked on me, her thighs tightening at my sides.

Her moans grew louder when I switched breasts, sucking the other nipple into my mouth, working it the same way I had worked the other, making it swollen and fat. I looked over at her other nipple, playing with it, rubbing it with my thumb. It was cherry red now, the skin around it pursed, making it stand out even further.

"God!" she cried when I pressed her breasts together, moving my tongue back and forth between her nipples, making a wet trail over her skin. Her hips were rolling on me fast now, making circles, grinding against my belly, her breath coming in short gasps.

She wiggled in my hands, almost like she was trying to get away, and her pussy edged further and further downward until her arse was nestled in the saddle of my hips and my cock was standing straight up, resting against the crack of her bum.

"Hey." I slid my hands down her sides. She was looking down at me, licking her lips, her eyes half-closed in pleasure. I slid my hand between her legs, feeling her wetness, sliding my finger under the elastic and teasing her clit. She whimpered and then moaned. "Take off your knickers."

She slithered off me and slid them down her legs. I pulled my boxers the rest of the way off, holding my hand out to her. Our eyes locked, and we both knew in that moment what was about to happen. The electricity of our knowing passed between us, like a low communication. It was like a slow buzz or hum that I could feel deep in my belly.

She leaned in and kissed me, sliding the full softness of her body over mine, and I tasted her sweetness again, like peppermint candy. Inching her hips downward until my cock was trapped between us, rock hard against her belly, she continued to explore my mouth with her tongue.

When she broke the kiss to sit up on me, she did something that surprised me. Unsnapping the hair slides on the side of her head, she tossed them over on the night table, and then she took the rubber bands off the ends of her plaits, wrapping them around her wrist.

I watched as she unplaited her hair, running her fingers through it, shaking her head and letting it go wild. It was kinky and wavy now, and when she leaned back over and kissed me, it hung over me like a curtain and tickled my cheeks.

Then she slid down between my legs, taking the elastic bands and wrapping them each twice around the base of my cock. I stared, open-mouthed. It was tight, but not uncomfortable.

"What—?" I couldn't get the words out, because she was licking and sucking the head now, making smacking noises with her lips.

"It's your first time." She crawled up me. "It will make you last longer. Otherwise you'll shoot your cum right away inside me."

I groaned at the thought of shooting my cum into her. Oh my God, the reality that I was going to fuck my stepsister, that I was going to come up inside of her cunt, made my cock jump and throb—or maybe it was the restricted blood flow there, now?

"I want you," she whispered against my mouth, rocking her hips on me. I could feel her pussy, wet and open, my cock working between her slit. It was almost like being inside of her and I suddenly realised that I wanted to be— deep, deep inside of her.

"I want your cock, David. Don't say no," Dawn pleaded, her eyes on mine as she reached between us and squeezed my shaft. I groaned at her touch, her little hand rubbing me up and down her slit. "Please don't say no. I couldn't stand it."

I shook my head and I could see the disappointment on her face. "No," I said quickly. "I won't say no. I want you, too."

She kissed me in response, her mouth slanting across mine, and I felt her positioning me between her legs, guiding me. The head of my cock was pressing against her, I could feel the soft give of her flesh, opening to me.

"Say it," she whispered against my mouth. "Tell me you want to fuck me."

I groaned, my voice shaking. "I want to fuck you." I rubbed her back, her hips, her body like a magnet for my hands. I couldn't seem to get enough of her flesh. I looked up into her eyes and saw what she wanted, and I said it, feeling my flush, "I want to fuck you, big sister."

She moaned, biting her lip and rewarding me as she rocked a little, moving her hips, and beginning to slide her pussy down onto my throbbing shaft.

"Oh God!" I grabbed her hips, feeling the smooth, tight tunnel of her cunt enveloping me as she slid further and further down. I groaned and jerked against her when she hit bottom. She wiggled there and I could feel the meaty head of my cock pressing into some impossibly soft tissue deep inside of her. "Oh my God!"

"Yes!" She sat up on me, her hands on my chest. I looked down and saw her pussy lips spread open around my shaft. I could feel her all around me, a tight, wet heat, and as if she'd read my mind, she squeezed her muscles there, making me moan.

"Oh God, Dawn," I gasped. I had imagined it would feel good, ten times, a hundred times better than my hand or her mouth—but I had never imagined anything like this.

Then, she began to move.

That's when I understood why she had used the elastic bands. The moment she started riding me, I wanted to come. Just looking up at her made me want it, the visual stimulation so intense I could feel my balls aching for release. I closed my eyes against it, the sight of her breasts bouncing and swaying, her hair falling over her soft, rounded shoulders, her hands holding herself steady on my belly, and oh God, the sight of my cock slipping up between her pussy lips, watching it actually disappear into her flesh! I could never have stopped from shooting my load into her, but somehow I couldn't, quite, like the pressure between my legs was almost too intense now.

My hands rode with her hips as she began to really start sliding up and down my shaft, the soft wetness of her cunt swallowing the length of me again and again. I peeked out, I couldn't help it, the sight of her was incredible. She reached down to rub her clit, and I saw her eyes closed, her head back. Her breath was coming faster, her hips rocking and rolling under my hands.

Elastic bands or no, I couldn't stand it much longer. She looked down at me, her eyes barely slits. I saw her smile a little, and it must have been at the look on my face.

"I love your cock, baby brother." She slid up on me until I was almost out of her, and then came all-l-l-l the way back down. She stopped there, catching her breath, still rubbing her clit in slow circles.

"I want you to fuck me." She climbed off me. I groaned when my cock lost contact with her pussy. I had never known such a feeling, such a driving animal force. I wanted to throw her down and shove it back into her.

"I thought I was!" I gulped, watching her crawl back onto the bed. She edged me over, getting up on her hands and knees.

"No." She lifted her arse up in the air. "I want to be fucked. Like this."

Oh bloody hell. It was like looking at the picture in my porn mag, my favourite one, her bum in the air, his cock sliding into her from behind. Except this was real. And the girl in front of me was my stepsister. My cock throbbed, and I saw that it was still slick from her juices, from base to tip. The elastic bands at the base made it a deep, dark red.

She put her shoulders to the bed and her hands on her arse, spreading herself open, showing me. It was like she was offering herself to me, and oh, crickey, I could actually see the little gape of her hole. My cock seemed to move forward all on its own at that sight. There was nothing that was going to keep me from being inside of her. I couldn't stop myself. I didn't care if it was my stepsister—hell, part of me was now actually willing to admit that I wanted her *because* she was my stepsister.

I positioned myself between her legs, sliding the head of my cock against that hot, pink hole. The anticipation was almost too much. I knew exactly what she felt like inside now, and I knew I could never get enough of that feeling. I felt bewitched by her pussy—damned, a condemned man, ruined for anything else but this.

"Wait." She looked back at me. "Take off the bands."

I did, wincing as I felt the constricted blood flow beginning again. My cock was tingling, like it had an itch it wanted scratched. I couldn't stop myself. It was like I didn't have any control over my own body. I grabbed her hips, sinking myself as deeply as I could into her flesh, and she gasped and wiggled under my hands, making me moan.

This was entirely different from having her on top of me. The motion, the sensation, the delicious friction between our legs. When I started moving inside of her, watching my cock disappearing, seeing her pussy lips moving around my shaft, I thought I'd died and gone to heaven—or hell. It really didn't matter anymore.

"Oh fuck yes!" Dawn reached her hand between her legs, and I knew she was rubbing at her clit. "Yes! Yes! Fuck me!"

I did. I couldn't possibly do anything else. I squeezed her hips and fucked her harder, and now I really knew what she meant when she said she wanted to be fucked. *I* was fucking *her* now, thrusting my cock into her over and over, the wet sound of her pussy and her moans and her writhing driving me on, faster, harder. It was like some primal thing had taken me over. A rational part of my brain had shut off and something brutish and carnal had come forth to take its place.

"Fuck me, little brother!" She moaned, and I felt her cunt squeezing me, the muscles pulling me tight. Hearing her say that, calling me her little brother, made my cock jump, and my balls tightened. I was so fucking close. I didn't even know how I'd lasted this long.

"Do you like fucking your sister's cunt?" She panted, moving back against me now, bucking and moaning. Her movements were driving me crazy. "Tell me, David. Tell me how much you love it."

"Fuck!" I felt my climax fast approaching. I knew what she wanted to hear and I wanted it, too. I didn't want to deny it anymore. I was fucking my stepsister and it was exactly what I wanted to be doing—now and forever, bucking together in an endless dance of wild, wicked lust.

"Yes, yes! God, I love fucking your hot cunt, big sister!" I shoved myself into her, grunting with every delicious thrust now. Looking down, watching myself go into her, was almost too much. I reached down to feel it, the stretch of her pussy sliding over my shaft, and felt faint.

I couldn't resist, looking down at the dark, puckered hole of her arse, seeing it winking at me every time I slammed into her again—I slid my finger over it, gently stroking.

"Oooooo!" She squealed, wiggling against my finger like she wanted it, and so I pressed it there, seeing just the tip disappear.

"Oh hell!" She really seemed to like it so I pushed it slowly in and out while I fucked her, and it wasn't long before she was making her little Dawnie noises. That was all it took for me, those little "uh-uh-uh's" that told me she was about to come.

"Dawn, I can't hold back!" I groaned, feeling something coming to a deep, rolling boil in my testicles.

"Oh God, yessss! Fill me with your hot cum, baby brother!"

I shuddered and bucked hard, my cock beginning to spasm inside of her. All around my shaft, her pussy was fluttering, her muscles tightening and releasing, like she was milking my cock as I poured streams of hot fluid into her, over and over and over.

My thighs were actually quivering, and I had to put my hand against the wall to keep from falling over. She was panting, flushed, and I stared down at her, breathless, too. I was loathe to pull out of her, but I had to sit back on my heels, still dizzy.

"Jesus!" I leaned my head against my arm on the wall and watched in awe as my cum began to slide out of her hole, slipping down her slit. My cock, spent and growing limp, jumped at the sight of it dripping slowly from her raised, open cunt down onto the sheet.

Dawn sat up, turning and crawling into my lap, and snuggling up close. I leaned back against the wall and held onto her, stroking her sweat-dampened hair. It was wavy and silky under my fingers.

Looking at her dungarees and trainers on the floor, I found myself remembering my dream, me sitting between Mum and Dad, watching her do a headstand and showing me her pussy. My face was flushed at the thought.

"Are you okay?" I kissed her hair, wondering what time it was and how soon Mum and Dad would be home.

"Mmmm." She snuggled up and fitted her head right under my chin. "More than okay."

"Me too." I realised in that moment that it was the truth.

"Want to do it again?" She wiggled in my lap.

I groaned, but her bum squirming like that against my thighs made my cock perk up almost immediately. I couldn't believe it, but it was true.

I'd fucked my own stepsister, and I knew I should feel ashamed—the part of me that was listening for Mum and Dad sure knew it. Still, another part of me had been awakened this afternoon, and that part wanted nothing except to keep doing what we were doing.

Maybe that was the trick of this whole thing. Was this my hell on earth? The more I had of her, the more I wanted? Maybe I really was doomed.

Chapter Seven

Mum decided to install a notice board in the kitchen so we could all "communicate more." I thought she was off her head and refused to use the thing, but Dawn kept putting notes up on it in her fat, girlish handwriting.

Gone to market

Out with Laurie at the cinema

I hardly noticed them anymore, but a name caught my eye while I was standing at the refrigerator, swigging milk out of the carton. I choked when I read it, milk dribbling down my chin and wetting my bare chest.

At the cinema with Ken. Be back... whenever. She had scrawled a big, fat smiley face in the corner with little devil horns on it.

I wiped at the milk with the back of my hand and put the carton back in the fridge, yanking the note out from under the pushpin. It was her handwriting all right.

That can't be right. Bugger-all if it wasn't, though. After all her mithering about Ken, she was off playing tonsil tennis with him in the back of the cinema, probably letting him feel her up—or worse. It was the "worse" that made me slam my bedroom door and tell Mum to sod off when she came up asking me what the matter was.

"Your dad and I are going out," she said, finally giving up on trying to pull it out of me.

"Fine!" I yelled into my pillow. Everyone was going out on a date except me. Great. Just great.

"David, what is the matter—?"

"Nothing!" I rolled over and glowered at her, my arms crossed over my chest. "Just go! Go and... go and have a good time!"

She gave me a hurt, puzzled look, but she shut the door and left me alone. And that was exactly what I wanted. I dug out an old copy of *The Hobbit* and tried to read, but the words just kept swimming in front of my eyes and an image of my stepsister would sneak in somehow. Unfortunately, the image of Ken kept coming into my head along with her.

I kept seeing him sliding a hand up her thigh, feeling the fat swell of her cunt through her skirt in the darkness of the cinema. Would she be wet, I wondered—as wet as she was with me—the gusset of her knickers slick, almost oily with her juices?

Fuck, that thought made my cock hard.

Not that it was uncommon, my imagining the degree of moisture that currently existed between my stepsister's legs. Lately, all I could think about was Dawn's pussy and how much I wanted it. I couldn't deny it anymore, even to myself—all I could do was try to resist the temptation.

But Ken—he didn't have to resist, did he? No. He could slide his cock into my stepsister's wet, waiting cunt without a twinge of guilt or regret. And would she like it? I knew how hot she was, how randy, how much she liked to be fucked and licked, how much she loved to come. She wouldn't say no—why would she? Why should she? She'd at least get down on her knees right there in the back of the cinema and suck him off while she played with herself. The thought of her hand up under her skirt diddling her clit made my cock pulse, pressed between the mattress and my belly, and I threw the paperback across the room with a groan.

"Blimey!" I was talking to no one at all as I threw open my bedroom door, listening for my parents. They were obviously gone already. "If she can get laid, so can I."

At least, that was the theory. I rang Will to see what trouble we might be able to get into tonight.

"Want to go down to the pub for a pint?" I asked, pulling on my jacket. I was going, whether he was or not.

"The Bulldog?"

"I'm leaving now."

"Right. Meet you there."

It was easy to meet Will at The Bulldog. Easy to sit down with a pint of Harp Lager and watch the girls walk by and talk about the firmness or size of each of their assets. The problem was, I kept comparing them to Dawn. Breasts not as big. Smile not as bright. Eyes not... hers. I tried drinking more and ordered another pint.

"David Watson! Is that you?"

The voice was vaguely familiar, but when I turned around and saw her, I knew immediately.

"Julie Entwistle." She was taller than I remembered, probably because of the heels, but mostly because we weren't in sixth form anymore. The dress she had on looked like she was poured into it. I couldn't help but wonder, when I glanced at the rather short hemline, if she still wore nothing under her skirts.

"It's so good to see you!" she gushed, giving me a hug and pressing her all grown up assets against my chest. They were considerable—which reminded me of Dawn. Julie, though, had dark hair and eyes and I figured her nipples were dark, too, not pink like my stepsister's. The thought of finding out, though, was compelling.

"Want a beer?" I offered, holding up the pint.

"Oh, I've already had too much!" Julie giggled as she squeezed down into the chair between me and Will. It was crowded and there wasn't a lot of room in here tonight. We all had to practically yell to hear each other.

"Then, by all means, have some more!" Will said with a grin. I raised an eyebrow at him and saw Julie checking him out.

"This is my friend, Will. Will, this is Julie Entwistle. We were in sixth form together."

"He always tried to look up my skirt." Julie gave me a sideways look.

"Did he, now?" Will got a clean glass from the bar and poured her a draft. She drank half of it in a few gulps and then licked her lips.

"It wasn't just me, you know," I said, defending myself. "Rumor had it Julie didn't wear any knickers. I was just trying to see if it was true."

"And was it?" Will cocked his head at her, still grinning.

Julie flushed, but she was smiling. "The truth is…" She leaned in and cupped her hand around Will's ear, whispering something.

"Is that so?" He grinned over at me and then glanced down at Julie's crossed legs, one tanned thigh over the other. I was wondering how she got so tanned, and that, too, reminded me of my stepsister… in her bikini… rubbing oil all over herself…

"No fair," I protested, nudging Julie under the table. "You can't tell him and not tell me."

"I just did." She winked as she stood, leaning in toward Will again and asking, "Want to dance?"

He stood up and let her lead him to the dance floor while I poured myself another draft and watched. So much for getting laid tonight. Julie clearly already had a thing for my best friend, and in spite of her considerable assets, I still couldn't keep my mind off my stepsister. Thinking about whether Julie was wearing knickers tonight just made me remember the smell of Dawn's when I picked them up in the washroom.

Christ, I was sick. I drank down the rest of my beer in three gulps and poured myself another. I needed to stop, and I knew it. The only thing that could keep my mind off my stepsister's cunt, I reasoned, was finding another one to take her place. I glanced around the pub, checking out the prospects. Fact was, Julie was one of the prettiest girls there, and since I already knew her, that was quite spawny. I could even offer to take her home, since Mum had said she and dad wouldn't be back until the next day—something about staying in a guest house overnight in Gatwick after some show.

Of course, that meant I was going to have to fight Will for her. I looked out at the dance floor and saw his hands already sneaking down past her waist toward her arse. Guess I was going to have to turn on the charm, I decided, downing another beer. I made up my mind, standing up and turning toward the dance floor, and that's when I saw them.

My height gave me a clear vantage point, and there was no mistaking her dirty-blonde hair and the mischievous smile she gave him over her shoulder. It was my stepsister, all right, leading Ken into the pub by the hand.

I sat back down, wondering if she had seen me, but she was clearly too interested in Ken. She stopped amidst the crowd for a minute, pulling his arms around her waist from behind and leaning her head back so she could say something into his ear. My eyes followed the long curve of her neck down the V of her white blouse, low-cut and showing off the tanned tops of her breasts. She had some red sparkly skirt on with shoes to match, like Dorothy from the Wizard of Oz, only I don't think Dorothy had ever worn anything so short and tight.

I sank into my seat as they passed, sure she would see me now, but no—she was a girl on a mission, leading Ken toward the dance floor. She'd clearly come to dance tonight, and wasn't letting him out of it, although I saw him give a lingering look toward the bar. He looked like he forgot all about it though, once they were out there. I maneuvered myself in my seat so I could watch Dawn wrapping her arms around his neck, rubbing up against him as the music pounded. It was 80's nostalgia night and Rick Springfield was wishing he had Jessie's Girl, and I rather knew how he felt. They were snogging, pressed up close, and even as far away as I was, I could have sworn I saw Ken's tongue in my stepsister's mouth.

I bit the inside of my cheek as I poured myself another beer, finishing off the pint. I told myself not to look, but I couldn't help it. Ken's hands were massaging my stepsister's arse through her skirt, pulling up the material, and if it weren't for the tables in my way, I was sure I could have seen her knickers. If she was wearing any. Was she wearing any? Fuck! I saw Julie dancing with Ken a few feet away, laughing at something he said. I stood up and threaded my way through the crowd, going around so Dawn wouldn't see me as I cut in between Julie and Will.

"You two look like you're having too much fun," I said, slipping between them and winking at Julie. I looked over my shoulder. "Pint's gone, Will—your turn to order."

He shrugged, heading back to the table, and Julie shook her head, putting her arms around my neck. She seemed amenable to the change in partners, and I was relieved. Now, if I could just focus on the girl in front of me, and not pay any attention to the one behind me in the red skirt...

"So what have you been up to since sixth form?" I asked, my hands finding the soft curve of her hips. She was a little thinner than my stepsister, but not too skinny, and I liked that. "Did you graduate?"

"With honours." She nodded "You?"

"By the skin of my teeth."

She laughed. "Too busy trying to look up other girls' skirts?"

I grinned. "Something like that."

Julie felt good in my arms and when the music turned slow, she snuggled closer, putting her head on my shoulder, and that felt good, too. It gave me a chance to look around, though, and that was a mistake. I saw Dawn and Ken swaying together in a similar posture—except Dawn's eyes were open and she was looking right at me. Something inside me froze, seeing the way my stepsister was watching us. She didn't make any sign of acknowledgment—she didn't move, she didn't even blink—but her eyes said it all.

"You feel nice." Julie tilted her head up, her eyes half closed and sleepy looking. I could smell alcohol on her breath—definitely more than beer—and knew she probably really had had way too much to drink.

"You feel nice, too," I admitted, letting my eyes flit toward Dawn once as Julie advanced. My stepsister was still watching, eyes wide and blazing. Then we were kissing, Julie's mouth soft and opening under mine, her body melting against me. I got lost in the sensation for a moment, I admit it, the press of her breasts against my chest, the curve of her hips moving under my hands. Even my cock

responded, growing thickly down my thigh as we danced—
that was, until I heard my stepsister's voice.

"Prick!"

I knew she was talking about me, even though it was
Ken she left on the dance floor as she turned and stalked off
toward the lav. The song was over and I stepped back,
looking down at Julie.

"Listen, I have to take a piss. Meet you back at the
table?"

"Sure."

I passed Ken at the bar. He was standing there ordering
a pint and didn't seem too concerned about my stepsister's
outburst. I found her in the lav, standing at the mirror
between two other women, putting on mascara. I didn't
think twice about going in after her, in spite of the wide-
eyes of the girl in the pink training suit who was leaving as I
burst in.

"David!" Dawn blinked fast, staring at me in the mirror.
"What in the hell are you doing in here?"

"Uh, wrong room," said the ginger next to my stepsister,
tucking her red hair behind her overly-pierced ears. "Blokes
are down the hall."

"Kenny Moore?" I sneered. "Like we both don't know
what he wants?"

"Look who's talking!" Dawn's eyes blazed again, that
same look I saw when she was watching me out on the
dance floor. "Julie Entwistle? She hasn't worn knickers
since we were all in primary!"

The two women on either side of her shrank back as we
fought, hustling quickly out the door.

"You do realise there's no vaccine against stupidity?" I
asked, folding my arms and frowning at her. "Besides,
Kenny Moore just wants to get into your knickers."

She glared at me, mascara in hand. "So? What if I want
him to?"

"Oh, so now you want him to? God, Dawn…" Our eyes
locked in the mirror, and mine were just as on fire as hers.

"You were the one crying to me about him the other night and now you're going to let him just... have you?"

"It's none of your business, David." She shoved the end of the mascara back in the tube, zipping it angrily into her makeup bag. Then she looked up at me, curling her lip in a half-smile, half-sneer. "You're *just my brother*... remember?"

"Right." I felt my jaw tighten and swallowed hard. "And you're such a slag you'll let anyone fuck you?" Her eyes widened at that as I stepped forward, trapping her against the sink. I could feel the swell of her bottom, the way her body was meant to bend over as I pressed my weight against her and hissed in her ear, "Even your own brother!"

She narrowed her eyes at me, shoving her makeup bag back into her purse and scowling. "Not anymore."

"The hell you won't." I grabbed her arm as she turned and tried to move past me. "If you're going to fuck Kenny Moore, you can damn well share some of it with me."

"David—"

I kissed her, hard, pressing her back against the sink, forcing her legs apart. She struggled at first, squirming in my grip as I shoved my tongue into her mouth, my crotch between her thighs. I was rock hard already and when Dawn started kissing me back, her arms going around my neck, my cock started leaking like the Coedety Dam.

"David, hurry," she urged, hiking her skirt up and pulling her knickers aside. They were red, too, like her skirt and her shoes. I groaned, seeing her cunt splayed open on the white porcelain as she rubbed herself. She watched me as I unbuckled my belt and shoved my jeans and shorts down my hips, gasping when my cock sprang free and reaching for it, squeezing, hard.

I wanted all of her and slipped my hand down into the V of her blouse as she stroked me, finding her nipple and squeezing it through her bra.

"Come on, baby brother," she tugged me closer, lifting her feet up and hooking her red heels in the edge of the sink.

This pushed her bottom out, and her pussy, too, opening it for me. "Take what you want—*if you really want it.*" Her eyes dared me, her voice low, and she licked her lips as she glanced toward the door. If anyone came in—

"Dawn..." I hesitated now, looking back over my shoulder, but then she slid the head of my cock between her lips, rubbing me up and down her slit. "Ohhhh God..."

"Here you go," she whispered, aiming me, pushing her hips up as far as she could. It was downright filthy, the way she was splayed out in the sink, and I reached in and grabbed her tits, pulling them out of her bra as I shoved forward, sinking my cock into her. The top button on her blouse popped open as I kneaded her flesh and when I glimpsed her heavy breasts overflowing their cups, I wanted more.

"David!" She hissed at me as I pulled her blouse open further, watching her tits sway as I fucked her, pounding myself deep into her pussy. I thumbed her nipples and she moaned, balancing herself on the sink with her hands behind her, lifting her arse to meet me. Her thighs were splayed, thick, the muscles quivering, and the juicy sound of her pussy was driving me crazy as I slid into her tight little crevice.

"Wait, wait," she gasped, arching, biting her lip as I grabbed her hips, driving my cock deeper. "I can't... like this... anymore..."

I pulled her forward, helping her down, kissing her hard as I did. Her tongue melted against mine, her body soft in my arms as I turned her around and bent her over the sink. The swell of her arse filled my hands as I shoved her skirt up over her hips and pulled her knickers down to her knees. She spread for me right away, arching her back and lifting her bottom, showing me what she wanted. I aimed my cock at her hole, watching in amazement as I disappeared into her, sliding forward until I was just gone, buried somewhere in the deepest, most secret part of my stepsister's body.

"Play with yourself, Dawnie," I urged, grabbing her hips and starting to fuck her. I wasn't going to last long at all—and that was probably a good thing, I wagered, glancing back at the door, which had still not opened... yet. "Make yourself come for me."

She whimpered as I slammed her into the sink, reaching underneath to find her clit, rubbing it fast and hard. Her face was a beautiful mask of pleasure in the mirror, her breath fogging it as she panted toward her finish line, her pussy squeezing me every so often, making my cock jerk in response. Just watching her touch herself made me want to come. I felt it building as she moaned and gasped, her tits completely out of her blouse and slapping against the faucets as I fucked her.

"Ohhhh fuccckkkk!" She whispered, her mouth open as she pressed her cheek against the mirror, her tongue sneaking to the corner of her mouth. "I'm gonna come for you, David. Oh God, baby... baby... nowwwww."

I felt it, the sweet shudder, the quivering spasms of her cunt around me as she came. I grabbed her hips and held her still on my cock, feeling my own orgasm hovering right at the edge. If I hadn't closed my eyes, the sight and sound of her together would have pushed me over. As it was, just the quivering edge to her voice as she came, the low tremble and tremor of her, nearly sent me.

"Dawnie," I warned, my fingers digging into her hips and arse. "Oh fuck, Dawn, I'm—"

She was quick, shifting her hips forward and turning to take me into her mouth before I knew what was happening. Now I could look at her, squatting on the washroom floor in her red heels, her skirt pushed up, her blouse open, her eyes big as she took my full length into her mouth. There was no holding back at the sight of her. I grabbed the back of her head, moaning as I thrust against the soft ease of her tongue, the sweet resistance of her palate.

She made soft noises as she began to swallow and I watched her through half-closed eyes, giving all my cum to her in huge, trembling waves. My hips bucked uncontrollably, my balls tight as they emptied themselves over my stepsister's eager tongue. She moaned and sucked me harder, making me shudder as she sucked me dry. My cock began to go almost immediately soft in her mouth.

"Dawnie, Dawnie," I whispered, easing myself back, pulling her up to me. I kissed her, grabbing her bottom, still bare under her skirt. "What are you doing here with him? I couldn't stand seeing you—"

"Don't." She kissed me back, quick and light, then pulled her knickers up and started tucking herself back in. I adjusted myself, too, pulling up my shorts and jeans, watching her run her fingers through her hair in the mirror.

"Don't what?" I swallowed, moving in behind her, putting my arms around her. She sighed, leaning back against me for a moment.

"You *are* my brother... remember?"

Her words cut me, reminding me of what I didn't want to be reminded of, and I took a step back. "So what now?"

I thought I saw her lip tremble, but she turned to me and said, "Now I go back out to my date... and you go back out to yours."

I shook my head, denying it. "That's... that's just bloody wrong, Dawn."

"No." She pressed her fingers to my lips. "This is."

I pulled away from her as she started to walk past me. "Then why doesn't it feel wrong?" I called.

"It does." She glanced over her shoulder at me, her expression caught between that mischievous Dawnie smile and something else, something sadder. "That's why it feels so good."

She pushed the door open and went out. I stood there for a minute, leaning against the sink, trying to remember how to breathe. When a little goth girl came into the washroom, she stood at the door with her mouth hanging open so far I could see her tongue stud. It wasn't until then I remembered where I was.

"What are you staring at, you bloody bint?"

I shoved past her and went out into the pub, determined not to look for my stepsister.

Chapter Eight

Julie was right in the middle of giving me such a bad blowjob—including teeth, a grip like a vice and a bruising Hoover-like suck—that it felt like she was going to pop the head of my cock like some blistered spot. I knew I was going to have to stop her and was just about to when she sat up and asked, "Where's the loo?"

"First door on your left." I was glad she had to go. It didn't just give my poor dick a break—it gave me time to think about ways to get rid of her. I could only vaguely remember her hanging on my arm earlier in the night while I watched my stepsister grind on the dance floor with Ken. When the pub closed down, and Dawn gave me her little finger-wagging wave on the way out, somehow Julie ended up tagging along after me while I trudged home, talking the whole while, although I'm not sure what about.

I heard a flush and sighed, yanking my jeans up over my waning cock. I knew it was crazy – I had a girl, a perfectly willing, more than sufficiently sloshed and decidedly randy girl – in my very own bedroom, and I was about to ask her to leave. And why? Because all I could do was think about my damned stepsister and the way she felt earlier all over me as I fucked her in the washroom of the pub? What kind of knob was I turning into?

"What are you doing here?" Dawn's voice carried clearly through my door and I bolted out of bed to find her standing in the landing, Ken coming up the stairs behind her. Julie blocked their way down the hall, her top still half undone. I noticed Ken noticing and gritted my teeth. "What the hell, David? Mum and Dad take a trip and you decide to turn the house into a knocking shop?"

I snorted, looking pointedly at Ken, and picked up an imaginary telephone. "Hello, Pot? This is Kettle. You're black."

Dawn had the decency to blush, at least. "Ken's place is… unavailable."

"Spraying it for fleas?"

"Shut up, David."

"Julie." I held my hand out to her and she smiled and melted rather nicely against me in the doorway. I enjoyed the look of fury on Dawn's face. "Let's get back to knocking."

"I'm telling Mum."

"You do that." I pulled Julie past me, into the room, and lowered my voice. "And I'll have lots of interesting things to tell Mum about my... *older*... sister... the one who's supposed to be looking out for her *baby brother*..."

She glanced back at Ken and then hissed. "You wouldn't."

"Try me."

I grinned as she stamped her foot, her hands balled into fists at her sides, but I shut the door before she could start her building tirade and shoved a chair under the door handle so she couldn't burst in. Julie sidled up behind me, wrapping her arms around my waist and taking steps back toward the bed.

"Don't you hate having a sister?"

"You have no idea."

She put her hand over my crotch and sighed. "You must be really ready to blow."

"You have no idea."

"Let me make you forget all about her."

I sighed. *Good luck with that.* "Let's give it a try."

Afraid to let her at my poor, aching cock again, I rolled her over onto her back as we kissed, sliding down and unbuttoning her top. She made happy noises and even helped me with her bra strap when I fumbled behind her back for the hooks. Her breasts were almost as full in my hands as Dawn's, but I was right about her nipples – small and dark, like little pebbles under my tongue. I pressed her tits together and buried my face between them, feeling a little dizzy, probably still more than a little drunk. I didn't want to admit, even to myself, that I was imagining my stepsister, the velvet feel of her skin, the way she gripped my hair, guiding me lower, lower…

"Oh David, yes." Julie whimpered and wiggled, but the sound of her voice broke my little trance, brought me back to the present, where it wasn't Dawn in my bed after all.

"SHH!" I urged her, a little too harshly, and she jumped. Even in the dark I could feel her draw back. "Sorry… It's just… my sister… down the hall…"

"Right."

"I'm sorry." I really was sorry. What was I thinking? Here was this girl, a nice girl by all rights, although a little bit slutty to be willing to do this on a first date – not even a date, really. But I could forgive her, considering we'd known each other so long. Here was this nice, willing girl, and I was feeling withdrawn and hateful. I lowered my head to her breasts again in apology, licking at her nipples. She sighed and arched, her breath coming faster as I sucked them into my mouth. I experimented, pressing them together, running my tongue back and forth between her nipples.

"Oh God! YES!"

Both of us froze at the sound of my sister's voice. It carried all the way down the hall, frenzied and loud. "Yes! Yes! YES!"

I blinked fast, glad for the darkness so Julie couldn't see the rising colour in my face. She would have mistaken it for embarrassment anyway, but it wasn't. I was furious.

Julie giggled. "And you thought *I* was being loud?"

"Fucking hell!" Gritting my teeth against my stepsister's moans, I pinched Julie's nipples, probably a little too hard, making her squeal. "You like that?" She yelped as I sucked one of them into my mouth, working the other one between my thumb and first finger, and then she moaned, her head going back, her hips pressing up against me.

I was furious with Dawn and taking it out on Julie, but I'm pretty sure the girl in my bed mistook my newfound fervour as passion and saw it as a welcome change from my former laissez-faire attitude. She grabbed my head, pressing me lower, lifting her skirt up over her hips. I heard my stepsister making that tell-tale "uh-uh-uh" and knew, whatever they were doing, that she was going to come. The thought made me crazy and I pressed my face between Julie's legs with a pained groan, finding the gusset of her knickers wet, the smell of her making me even more dizzy.

"Yes, Davey," Julie whispered. It was the name they used to call me in sixth form–the name my stepsister used when she teased me. "Yes, yes, please, lick it, please…"

I yanked the material aside, exposing the soft, dark down of her pubic hair. I was grateful she wasn't shaved smooth – I didn't want any more reminders of Dawn.

"Tell me," I insisted, parting her lips with my fingers, hearing her whimper. "Tell me you want it."

"Oh God." Her hips rocked up toward my mouth. "Please, yes. I want it. I want it!"

My stepsister was getting fucked. I knew the steady, staccato sound of her voice, rising with her orgasm, as a cock slammed into her again and again. That little weasel was fucking my stepsister. Never mind that I wanted to be that bloke – never mind that I *had* been that bloke, earlier tonight, rutting between my own stepsister's legs like some wild boar that didn't know the difference between food and rubbish. What was I turning into? My cock ached, listening to the rolling rise of her voice, the sweet catch in it, the way it lowered when she begged, "Fuck me hard! Harder! Come on! Come on!"

Was she thinking about me, I wondered? And what if she wasn't? The thought made me go cold inside, remembering what she'd said earlier, about how wrong what we were doing really was. As if I didn't know that? As if I hadn't agonised over it from the beginning? Now that *I'd* given in, *she* was…

It came to me that she was doing this on purpose—being loud, putting on a show—to prove something? But what?

Julie wriggled out of her knickers, spreading her legs wide again, inviting me with every rock and sigh. Listening to my stepsister was making me insane with jealousy and lust. I wanted to go down there, burst into the room, kick Ken's whiny little arse from one end of the room to the other, and then give my stepsister the spanking she deserved—but I knew I couldn't. I knew I shouldn't even be thinking about it, shouldn't even care. But I did. Far too much.

The girl whose legs were spread for me seemed to notice my hesitation, sense my dilemma. *God, I hope not.* I couldn't see her face in the dark, but she was quiet now, her breathing slower. I made a decision, then and there, that I was going to make Julie feel so good she'd scream with pleasure—and maybe, just maybe, give Dawn a little dose of her own medicine.

"Louder," I urged, parting her lips again with my fingers. "Tell it to me louder."

I don't know if she understood. Part of me thought she did, from the way she froze for a moment, her breath caught—but she did it anyway. That act alone excited me.

"Lick my cunt!" she insisted and I knew her voice was carrying down the hall, all the way into my stepsister's bedroom. I smiled in triumph, lowering my face to Julie's waiting pussy, my tongue parting the soft folds of flesh, searching for her clit.

"Oh yes," she whispered, lifting her hips to my mouth. Then her hands were in my hair, mashing my lips and tongue against her, grinding her wetness against my face, and her voice rose louder, no longer asking or begging, but insisting, demanding. "Lick it! Yes! Oh God! Don't stop! Make me come!"

That was my plan, of course, but it was out of my hands, now. Julie was using me, my mouth, taking herself there, and every word and moan reverberated through me. I was all tongue for her, letting her rub herself against my face, and I found myself unzipping my jeans, stroking my throbbing cock through the material as she twisted against me.

I couldn't hear my stepsister at all now as Julie thrashed and bucked on my bed, and I was so relieved I might have sworn eternal loyalty to her or some such rot if she'd asked me in that moment. The girl was coming, and coming hard, her moans filling my head as she flooded my mouth with the sweetness of her cum. She rubbed herself off on my face until I couldn't breathe and didn't care, and then she pulled my head back, still panting from her climax, and whispered, "Now... let's give them a real show. Get up here and fuck me."

Hardly believing what I was hearing, I crawled up between her legs, my face smeared with her juices, and she kissed me, sucking my tongue deep into her mouth as she wrapped her legs around my waist. Her hand was searching between us and I helped her, shoving my jeans down, groaning when she wrapped her fingers around my cock.

"Julie..." I said her name, like an apology, and somehow I think she knew it, but it didn't matter. She was going to give me what I wanted—and I was grateful for that, too. She guided me into her wetness and it was like sliding through butter. Wiggling underneath me, she arched and pressed into the saddle of my hips, digging her bare heels into my lower back to make me fit more perfectly inside of her. Her muscles were taut and stretched around my cock, making me heady with the sensation, eager to thrust toward completion, but I held back, caught between my desire and my fear of where it might lead.

"Come on! Give me that big, hard dick!" Julie's nails dug into my back as she began to move underneath me, her body twisting and turning in my arms. I gave her what she wanted. Not just because she wanted it—and it was clear to me she really did—or even because I wanted it, but because I knew my stepsister was listening. I could *feel* her listening, could sense the rising colour in her cheeks, the troubled pallor underneath.

As much as I later would have liked to say I fucked Julie that first time because I really wanted her, it wasn't about that in the least. I fucked her because I wanted to be fucking my stepsister—I wanted to make Dawn jealous, wanted her to wish it was my cock thrusting into her, my mouth muffling her moans as I rode her squalls of pleasure.

And Julie put on quite a show. She gave such an outstanding performance I couldn't tell anymore whether she was acting or not when she threw her head back and called my name, begging me to fuck her harder, faster, deeper, more, more, more... I didn't know until I felt her cunt spasm, actually felt her muscles flutter and tighten around my prick as she reached her climax and I realised this was no act, at least, not anymore. She was coming under me, shuddering, biting my shoulder to keep in her screams, which came anyway, wails of pleasure torn out of her throat with every thrust.

And Dawn was yelling at my door, knocking fast and hard, thrusting against the chair I'd propped there to keep anyone out. "David! Christ! The bloody neighbours can hear you!"

"Fuck off!" I gasped, looking down into Julie's pained expression, the exquisite torture etched there making me feel protective and affectionate all of a sudden. I wanted to scoop her up, crawl inside her, die. And I hadn't even come. Wasn't going to, either. I pulled out, collapsing next to her on the bed as she purred like a kitten and cooed like a pigeon, curling her soft body against mine. I rolled to my side, hiding my still throbbing erection, letting her spoon against me and pull the covers up.

"How was that?" she murmured, kissing my shoulder blade, the tickle of her nails along my side as she slid an arm under mine a sweet reminder of her femininity.

"A stellar performance, ta." God, that was mean. I realised it right away and meant to take it back, but I didn't know how. Still, she didn't say anything. Neither did my stepsister. Dawn had given up and gone away – or was still listening outside the door

Either way, it didn't matter. I closed my eyes against all of it, my head spinning, and slipped toward sleep.

* * * *

The ache of beer sitting in my bladder like a thousand stone woke me up, and I slid out from under Julie's arm, stumbling toward the bog in the dark. The edge of the chair was still wedged under the door and I set it aside. Everything was quiet, the hallway a dark tunnel as I felt my way.

I shut the door and turned on the light out of habit. Mum insisted my aim at the toilet bowl was bad enough during the day, let alone at a sleepy two in the morning darkness. I was mid-stream in a heavy flow, my kidneys ridding themselves of the copious amounts of alcohol I'd consumed all night, when the door opened. I'd forgotten to lock it. Afraid it might be Ken, I turned my back towards the door, calling over my shoulder, "Give me a minute!"

"Just one?" The door snicked closed and my stepsister turned the lock behind her.

I shook off, my heart hammering, and dropped my shirt to cover myself—my shorts and trousers were in my room—turning to face her. She was wearing Ken's shirt, navy blue button down, open from neck to the tail ends that hung almost to her knees.

"Jesus, Dawn—don't you know how to knock? What if it had been Julie in here?"

"So what if it was?" My stepsister cocked her head at me, her eyes slightly narrowed as she slid up onto the counter while I turned on the tap to wash my hands. "I'd like to have a talk with that skank."

"Look who's talking." I reached across her to dry my hands and she grabbed my arm, pulling it around her back.

"What makes me more of a slut?" she whispered, hooking her bare foot behind my knee and spreading her

- 100 -

legs to pull me in close. "Letting Ken take my arse tonight or me wanting to fuck my own brother?"

My breath caught and I chided my cock for rising at the thought of my stepsister's arse in the air, that puckered hole she had asked me to finger waiting for the plunge of something much larger and demanding. It wasn't listening, though, my cock. It had a mind of its own. It knew just what it wanted—and what it wanted was sitting right here splayed on the washroom counter in the treacherous form of my stepsister.

"Come on, baby brother." Dawn slipped her arms around my neck, her breath hot against my ear. "Enquiring minds want to know. Which is worse?"

"Dawn..." I swallowed and closed my eyes as she shifted, hooking her other leg around me and snuggling her crotch right up against mine. "God..."

"I was thinking about you the whole time."

Her whispered words stopped everything inside of me. It was what I'd been afraid of and secretly – or not so secretly – hoping for. I slid my arms around her waist, under Ken's shirt, which reeked of some awful cologne and was giving me a headache. Her skin was soft as down and I wanted to bury every part of myself in it.

I almost choked on my own words. "I was thinking of you, too. I couldn't help myself."

She sighed and melted in my arms, turning her face up to be kissed. I hated the thought of her mouth anywhere near the twat sleeping right now in her bed, but I didn't taste a trace of him on her when I slipped my tongue in to touch hers. She tasted just like she always did—sweet, a little like almonds and honey—and I had a feeling she hadn't, at any point, kissed Ken tonight like she was kissing me now, her mouth hungry and eager, her hands roaming all over my body as if making sure I was real, solid, and here to stay. At least, I hoped she hadn't.

"Did you like his cock in your arse?" I bit the words off, each one, leaving angry red love bites on her neck as I pulled the shirt down over her shoulders. She slipped her arms out of the sleeves, lifting my shirt off so she could press herself fully against me, her breasts flattening against my chest as her mouth sought mine again.

But I wouldn't kiss her. Instead, I cupped her chin, squeezing her mouth with my thumb and first finger, tugging gently at her lower lip. "Answer me. Did you like his cock in your tight little arse?"

I'd seen plenty of pictures of anal sex—*Naughty Bits* did a whole issue devoted to it once—but I don't think my stepsister knew how much I'd thought about it, how that sweet, dark hole intrigued and called me into its humid depths. The thought of my stepsister's arse up in the air being fucked made me want to bend her over right now and shove it into her with a force that would wake both Julie and Ken and make Dawn wail.

"Why? Are you jealous?" Her tone was teasing as she jerked her head out of my hand and reached between us, grabbing onto the steel length of me and squeezing out a torturous rhythm.

I rolled my eyes convincingly—I hoped. "Why should I be jealous of him? The guy's all foam and no beer."

"What's that supposed to mean?"

I snorted. "His chimney's clogged…he doesn't have all his Weetabix in one box…his lift doesn't go all the way to the top…he forgot to pay his brain bill…"

"David, stop!"

"You deserve better than him. Kenny Moore is living proof that evolution can go in reverse!"

She tried to look cross, but she couldn't help smiling. "Well… I have to admit, his aerial doesn't pick up all the channels…" Dawn giggled and even I had to grin at her attempt to play my game. "But he's a good kisser."

That did it. I grabbed her bottom and pulled her off the sink, crushing her mouth to mine. She tried to gasp, breathe, something, but I wouldn't let her, my tongue probing hers, my hands spreading her arse cheeks, kneading her flesh with my fingers. We parted breathless, and I looked down into her glazed eyes for a moment, waiting for her to say something. Instead, she sank to her knees and took me into her mouth.

"Oh God, Dawnie…"

Her tongue ran like silk around the sensitive head of my cock, her fingernails tickling the hair on my balls, her other hand stroking me as she began to suck, the mischievous tilt of her eyes never leaving mine. I could have watched her suck me forever—the pink slide of her lips taut around my shaft, the stretch of her tongue to reach my balls when she took all of me in, the reddened swelling of her mouth as she rubbed the head against her cheek before taking me again— could have watched her until she made me shoot the load I'd been saving for her all night right down that sweet, swallowing little throat. But Dawn had other ideas. Better ideas. And who was I to argue?

"I heard you fucking her…" My stepsister whispered her words as she outlined her mouth with the head of my cock like she was using a lipstick tube, spreading my precum over her lips. "Did you like her pussy, baby brother? Did she make you come hard?"

I didn't want to think about the girl sleeping in my bed. I didn't want to admit to my stepsister that I'd had sex with anyone else but her, and the absurd, twisted paradox of it threatened to make my skull explode as Dawn stood and let me taste the pre-cum gloss on her lips.

"Did you like hers as much as mine?" She brought my hand between her legs and the heat there threatened to burn my palm as I cupped her bare flesh and slid a finger into her wetness. She sighed and shifted her hips forward, leaning her hands back against the counter and already involuntarily trying to fuck my hand, her eyes half-closing. She was the most beautiful thing I'd ever seen, before or since, and I wanted her more than I was willing to admit, even to myself. I couldn't resist, and there was no point trying. I sank to my knees and pressed my face to her pussy, the motion of my lips and tongue making her gasp and then moan and rock against me.

"You licked her, didn't you?" Dawn's hands moved in my hair as she eased her bottom onto the sink and spread her legs wider. "You ate her hot, wet little cunt until she came all over your face, didn't you, Davey?"

I made a muffled, choking noise against her flesh and then sucked the tiny nub of her clit into my mouth, making her head go back, a low growling sound coming from her throat. She tasted like a fig, just as wrinkled and puckered, too, my tongue finding its way through the folds in her flesh. I thought she was going to give me her come, let me take it, draw it out of her like a bee's search for a sweet meal, but Dawn had, as I said, other ideas. Better ones.

"I bet she didn't let you fuck her arse, did she?"

I groaned, even with my tongue pressed into the juicy hole of her pussy, my nose rubbing up against her clit. She pulled my head back, my face smeared with her juices, and slid down to stand onto the floor again. Her eyes were on mine, that mischievous look back in them again, a light I'd come to recognise and love.

"But you'd like to get your prick into a tight little arsehole, wouldn't you?" Her thumb rubbed her wetness over my lips and chin, her eyes following her fingers' trail. "Especially if it was your own sister's tight little arsehole... wouldn't you, baby brother?"

I couldn't speak. I could barely think. The only thing leading me was the hot throb of my prick, pointing straight up from my lap like an arrow pointing the way as my stepsister turned around and bent over the sink. When she opened her legs, reaching both of her hands back to spread her cheeks, I saw it all – the swollen, fleshy part of her pussy lips, the pink glistening through, and especially the fluted pucker above it, winking at me like a teasing promise.

"You want that?" She furrowed her arsehole, squeezing her muscles and releasing. "Tell me, baby brother. Tell you want to fuck your sister's arse." I groaned as she pressed one of her fingers to that groove, watching as the tip disappeared. My cock drooled at the sight of it and I gripped it tight, as if I could keep it collared.

"Dawnie…"

She fucked the pucker of her arse with one finger, her eyes watching me for a reaction. I felt dazed, sick with my own lust, but my cock didn't care. Never mind that the girl I'd brought home was still asleep in my bed, and the bloke I'd heard my stepsister fucking was just down the hall. Never mind we were shut up in the loo. Never mind that the arse in front of me belonged to my own stepsister. My cock wanted what it wanted, and I knew we were going in.

"Wait!" Dawn squealed as I pressed the mushroom head of my prick between her open cheeks. She whirled around, her eyes wide, wagging a finger in my face. She looked so much like she used to when I was a tot that for a moment I froze. I flashed to the time she took me to the corner shop and caught me stealing, and I was so lost in the memory that, for a moment, I didn't even register what she was saying. "Don't ever try to put your cock into a girl's arse without lubing up first, you twat!"

Before I knew what was happening, she grabbed a bottle of lotion off the washroom counter, rubbing the thick stuff between her fingers to warm it before slathering it over my prick. I groaned, watching as she worked it up and down my shaft like a salve with her greasy hands. She was still shaking her head and muttering to herself about how daft I was, just like she had when she dragged me back to the store to apologise for stealing, yanking at my dick now like she'd yanked at my hand then, urging me to keep up.

That memory stayed, superimposed on the moment, and I remembered how long her strides had been, how shiny and blonde her hair was in the sun as she swung it over her shoulder and looked down at me with that sharp, disapproving look in her eyes. I'd never wanted to please anyone else more than in that moment and was filled with the shame of disappointing her. I didn't care so much about the sweets in my pocket or even that it was wrong to steal – which, of course, I knew. My longing had overcome my young moral sense. I'd wanted it so much, had stood there shifting my weight from foot to foot while my stepsister turned the pages of a teenager's magazine from the rack and I just ached for it.

Just like I'm aching for her, now.

I watched, feeling as if time had slipped into some sort of lapse, as my stepsister stood, just as tall and beautiful as she'd been then, and leaned in to kiss me. My body was shaking in anticipation, and although I was taller than she was now, I still felt young as she instructed me on what to do and how to do it, turning to bend over the sink again.

"You have to go slow, David. Slowwwww." She dragged the last word out, glaring over her shoulder. "Do you hear me?"

Her voice was chastising, the quintessential older sister, and I nodded my head earnestly, not trusting my voice. I thought it would come out in a squeak or the tenor of my youth, before my voice changed. I pressed the head of my cock against my stepsister's arsehole and remembered that moment, wanting it, longing for it, aching. I didn't have any money left and she wouldn't buy it for me and so I'd taken it. Just slipped it into my pocket—a secret, shameful, burning delight.

My mistake was taking it out to admire it before we got home. I thought Dawn was too involved with her magazine, but I was wrong. She saw it out of the corner of her eye, and although I stuffed it quickly into my pocket again before she could turn her head, she knew.

"Oh! God! Easy, David!" Dawn's voice drew me back to the present and I looked down to where her trembling hands held her buttocks open as I inched my way in. I could see my stepsister's face in the mirror as she bit her lip, her eyelids fluttering closed and then open again, her eyes trying to focus on mine. "Feels so… *big!*"

Flushing with an instant feeling of pride, I still hesitated, worried about her. "Does it hurt?" I asked, and began to pull back, but she shook her head, arching and pressing against me, forcing the head of my cock to inch further in, making me groan at the sensation. It was so *tight!*

"Don't stop!" She insisted, spreading herself even wider, the softly fluted hole of her arse accepting me in little flutters, the feel of it around my cock like the hottest, tightest little mouth in the world. I stood transfixed, wondering at the darkness I was slowly sinking into, when Dawn gave a sharp gasp and reached back with both hands to grab my hips and pull me into her completely.

"Ohhhhh fuck!" I wasn't expecting it and just the knowledge that my cock was buried in my stepsister's arse nearly made me lose it right then and there. Add to that the swell of Dawn's quivering behind settled into the saddle of my hips, her greasy hands gripping my thighs, and the way her breath fogged the mirror as she begged me to fuck her— "Fuck my arse! Do it! Do it!"—and it was almost hopeless. The only way I could keep from coming was to close my eyes, throw my head back, and remember the feeling of disappointing my stepsister that day, the critical look on her face, the shame of returning to the shop, my sweaty, nervous little hand tucked into hers.

"Dawn," I croaked, gripping her hips. "Hold still." Thank God she did as I asked. I took a few deep breaths before daring to open my eyes and meet hers in the mirror. She had that sly smirk, that mischievous look, and that's when I felt the tight hole of her arse squeezing itself around my cock. "Oh God... Dawn..."

"You like being in my arse?" She was teasing, the pink tip of her tongue raking over her teeth as she flipped her hair over her shoulder and glanced back at me. "Is that tight, baby brother? Is that nice and tight and hot around your big cock?"

"Yes!" I groaned, leaning into her and sliding my hands down into the V of her crotch. "You know it is."

"Yesssss..." She smiled, meeting my eyes in the mirror and wiggling back against me. "And I love you in my arse... feels so much better than Kenny's wee little thing..."

She knew exactly what her words were doing to me. My fingers found the soft, open part of her pussy lips, seeking the hard nub of her clit. She sighed and shifted, letting me know I'd found it, moving her hips in delicious circles and forcing my cock deeper inside of her. "Ahhh yes, yes... that's it..."

"You really like it?" I searched her eyes in the mirror, seeking her approval, her assent, and found it. She rocked back against me, spreading her legs wide to allow me to rub her clit faster. She was beautiful bent over the washroom sink, propped up on her elbows, her heavy breasts swaying as I started to really fuck her. God, but that hole was tight! The head of my cock deliciously grazed the hot, spasming band of muscle before sinking deep again. My stepsister's eyes fluttered closed and opened again, her cheek resting against the mirror, her breath making a fine mist over its surface as she moaned softly with each stroke.

"Yes, baby," she whispered, tilting her hips, an offering, a question – More? More? "Oh God, baby brother, I was thinking about you the whole time..." Our bodies slapped together now, my cock sinking deep into her tight channel, the lotion she'd coated me with easing the way, and still, it was so snug! "I was wishing it was you... oh Davey, I wanted you. I wanted *your* cock in my arse. I wanted this... I wanted this..."

"I wanted it, too." My admission burned through me. "I want you. All of you. All the time. I can't stop... God, Dawn, you're..."

"Harder, David!" she insisted, rolling her hips, driving me on. I wasn't going to be able to hold out much longer. The sweet pull of her arse, that shockingly stretched dimple of flesh swallowing my cock again and again, was sending me past the point of reason or thought or anything but pure sensation. She had given it to me, had longed for me, wanted me, ached for this as much as I had, and now she submitted completely and lost herself. I couldn't argue, I couldn't resist, I couldn't do anything but surrender to her lust and my own.

And so I did the only thing I could do—I fucked her harder, driving both of us toward a delicious finish, her little clit swollen against my fingers. I wanted to bury all of myself into her, climb inside her somehow, and I shoved my fingers into her pussy, making her gasp and writhe. I felt my cock slipping into her arse, felt it through that thin barrier of flesh, and groaned at the sensation.

"Oh fuck, oh fuck, oh fuck!" She repeated it over and over, her eyes unfocused, her tongue sneaking out to touch the corner of her mouth. She rubbed her cheek against the coolness of the mirror, her lips pressing there, too, as if she were kissing herself, or some smooth, one-dimensional twin. The sight was incredibly hot and I felt that delicious buzzing in my balls, the sweet tightening that meant there was no going back.

"Dawnie, I'm gonna come," I groaned, working the head of my cock back and forth at the hot opening of her arse. "Can I...? Can I...?"

"Come in my arse!" Her hands pressed, palms flat, against the mirror and she arched her back. "Fill my arse, baby brother! Fill it with all your hot cum!"

There was no stopping it. My cock slid deep as her hand covered mine, rocking her pussy against my fingers, bringing herself off, too. I felt her spasms, her pussy clamping down on my fingers, drawing them in, while her arsehole contracted, as if trying to push me out. This paradox was delightful, my cock caught right in the middle of the exquisite mesh of it all, pushed and pulled to the brink.

I growled low in my throat as I felt the first surge, coming up deep from my pelvis and finally spewing in delicious jets from the end of my cock, filling the dark, hot cavity of my stepsister's arse. Our bodies melded together in that moment, both of us quivering with sensation, Dawn's sweet climax coming in bursts like sunspots, almost blinding in their beauty. I closed my eyes to it and ground my hips into hers, unable to stop the wicked pleasure that flooded through me as I filled the most secret part of my stepsister's body with my cum.

I could barely stand—my legs still shook with the force of my orgasm. Dawn's body was sticky, and so was mine, but her skin gave off a bronze heat, and she was like velvet in my arms when she turned and wrapped her arms around my neck, giving me a long, soft, sweet kiss. I just held her, both of us still breathing hard, pretending that the washroom was some other world, not connected to our house or the people who lived in it—us included.

"We need to stop doing this." Dawn's eyes met mine. She looked sad and her words made me want to double over in pain.

Instead, I buried my face in her neck and breathed in her musky scent, and used an oft-repeated and used sibling phrase between us, only half joking, "You started it."

Dawn laughed. It bubbled up from the softness of her belly and made me shiver with its light. "You're a brat."

"It's all your fault." I feathered kisses over her collarbone, amazed and bemused that my cock was stirring again at the feel of her in my arms. "You started it, and now I can't stop…"

"I know." She sighed, this time in pleasure, as she tilted her head back for my kisses. "I don't want to stop, either."

"You don't?" I lifted my head to meet her eyes and saw that it was true. The realisation sunk in and I swallowed, glancing at the door and for the first time in a while wondering if someone might be standing on the other side of it, aghast at what they had heard.

"I don't." Dawn shook her blonde head, biting her lip. "I want you, David. I can't stop… wanting you."

I closed my eyes again and pulled her close. "What are we going to do?"

"I don't know." Her voice was a whisper and she buried her face against my chest. "I just don't know."

Chapter Nine

"David, who is this Julie who keeps ringing?"

"Mum, please!" I groaned and pulled the sofa cushion over my head. Dad was gone to a football game—I had declined the invitation for the sole purpose of catching forty-winks while no one rode me about a job. I'd flopped on the sofa with the pretence of watching a bit of the telly and had soon dozed off.

"That's Davey's new little bit o'fluff!" Dawn flew around the corner from the kitchen, carrying a bowl of Weetabix and dribbling milk down her chin onto the tops of her exposed, tanned breasts.

"Piss off!" I peeked around the cushion and glared at her, but it was hard to stay mad, watching the white liquid slide down her cleavage. It reminded me instantly of the way my cum looked covering her breasts and that made my cock jump.

Bloody hell! I shook my head to clear it, rubbing my eyes and blinking. I was just sick! Sick sick sick. And Mum was looking right at me. I was thinking about shooting cum all over my stepsister's tits and Mum...

Christ! I needed help.

"Don't you want to talk to your girlfriend, Davey?" Dawn smirked, wrinkling her nose at me.

"Girlfriend?" Mum folded her arms and frowned between us. Just the look in Mum's eyes made me feel guilty – even though she knew nothing about what Dawn and I had been doing together.

"Davey's dating no-knickers-Entwistle," Dawn informed her, wiping her chin with her fist. I rolled my eyes and threw the cushion at her. She laughed and sidestepped it rather gracefully, not even upending her cereal bowl.

"She's better than Ken the Knob-end," I snarled, getting up and pushing past both of them. "Can't you two leave a bloke alone for five minutes?"

"David!" Mum's tone stopped me at the landing. "Your no-knickers girlfriend is on the phone."

"Now?" I ducked back down to look at her. "Right now?"

"Why do you think I interrupted your cat-nap?"

I bounded back down the stairs and ignored Dawn's raised eyebrows as I stumbled my way to the kitchen. Our phone wasn't the cordless sort – it was one of those with the long, curly, stretchy cords, and I dragged it with me to the larder and shut myself in with the biscuits and blackcurrant jam.

"Jules?"

"Hey sexy." Just the sound of her voice made something warm spread through my belly. "Are we still on for tonight?"

I looked at my watch. "Seven, right?" Crickey, I'd slept longer than I thought!

"I can't wait." Her voice dropped a little, and I knew she was talking from work. She had a cushy job in a posh office as a front desk clerk, and I kept asking her to get me in. "Guess what I'm not wearing?"

"You are very naughty." My cock throbbed and I rubbed it through my trousers. I could imagine the exposed triangle of her cunt, just waiting to be parted by my fingers, my tongue. It made my mouth water.

"You have no idea." Her voice was low and teasing.

"You better stop." I grabbed a box of biscuits off the shelf, trying to distract myself. "You're making me hard."

"I should hope so!" Julie laughed – I was beginning to love her laugh. She was an incredibly fun girl, and she laughed a lot.

"Davey!" Dawn whinged, pounding on the larder door, trying to get in, but my back was to it. "I need the phone!"

"Buggar!"

"Go on." Julie was still laughing. "I just wanted to remind you about tonight."

"Definitely."

She lowered her voice again, this time to the sweetest whisper. "Miss you."

"I miss you, too."

When I pulled open the larder door, Dawn was standing there, hand out for the phone. She mimicked me as I gave it to her. "I miss you tooooooo."

"Shut up!" I stalked past her, unable to keep my eyes from dipping down to the delicious swell of her breasts. "And put some damned clothes on!"

"Mum!" My stepsister appealed to our mother, who was standing at the sink washing up.

Mum didn't even look away from the dishes. "Dawn, you really should get dressed some time today."

"I'm trying to get a tan!" Dawn adjusted her top – blimey, she had fantastic tits! Then she started dialing the phone.

"Looks like you've succeeded," I grumbled, sitting down at the kitchen table with the paper and trying not to notice how her suit rode up, revealing a thin line of pale skin around the edges. The rest of her was a beautiful bronze.

"Ken?" Her voice changed instantly as she cradled the phone against her ear. "Hi sweetie, I got your message, you said to call—"

I flipped idly through the paper, my trusty notebook beside me. Dad was due home soon.

"But I thought..." Dawn's finger twirled the cord. She turned away from both of us. Mum was done washing up and slipped out the back door. I heard the low rumble of Ken's voice through the receiver, but it was just a buzz – I couldn't hear any real words. Dawn's head lowered and she tried to say something – but it came out in a breathy, unidentifiable vowel sound as she leaned against the counter, still facing away from me.

I circled an ad, pretending I wasn't listening, pretending I didn't care. She was quiet for a long time—a long, long time. Finally, I gave up pretending and just stared, waiting.

"Fine then." That was all she said before she turned around and put the phone back. When she turned to me, her face was three shades of pale—not easy to do with the tan she'd managed to get in the past two weeks. "We aren't going out tonight."

I nodded, but I didn't say anything.

"We're not going out any night, ever again." She crossed her arms and leaned back against the counter, and for a minute, she looked all for the world like Mum when she was off her head. "He's back with his ex."

I wanted to go to her, hug her, tell her it was going to be okay, and just generally be as brotherly as possible. But another part of me... I couldn't believe how relieved I felt – how jealous I had been of that fuckwit. The thought of him touching my stepsister made me balmy, but more than that – it was the thought of *him* touching her instead of *me* that made me totally hatstand. I sat there, struggling with these two parts, the part of me that loved my stepsister the way I always had – as the girl who teased a lot but let me tag along when I wanted – and the part of me that had been fucking her at every possible turn for the better part of a week.

I'm pretty sure that's why I said what I did.

"I told you he was a scrote!"

She burst into tears and ran from the kitchen. I listened to the sound of her feet pounding up the stairs with a sick, sinking feeling in my gut. Mum came in then, and didn't know what had happened, so she started talking to me about how well her flowers were doing this year. I just nodded and circled random ads and tried to quell the burning in my mid-section. Later, Dad would ask me why I'd circled an ad for a trolley dolly and another one for a dental assistant, but by then, it wouldn't really matter.

I pushed off from the table and stood. "I've got to get ready to go out."

"With Julie?" Mom looked up from where she was arranging roses in a vase.

"We're going to a club." I didn't wait for her response. Upstairs, Dawn's door was closed, and I stood outside it and thought about knocking, about what I should say, what I was going to say. Finally, I just opened the door and went in without knocking at all, sitting on the edge of her bed.

"I'm sorry." I touched her back, the feel of her skin like satin under my fingers as I rubbed her shoulderblade, not knowing what else to do. She was still wearing her bikini. I expected her to yell at me, to tell me to get the hell out in her usual big-sister way. Instead, she rolled to her back and reached for me, her eyes wet from crying. When I saw that, my heart melted and I pulled her into my arms, stroking the soft gold of her hair. She clung to me, trembling and we stayed like that for a while, the silence heavy with possibility.

"I never really liked him." Dawn sniffed, snuggling her head under my chin. "Not any more than you like that manky Julie Entwistle."

I blinked at the wall, swallowing but not responding. The fact was, I did like Jules. I liked her a lot. But I couldn't say that, not now. After a moment, I felt my stepsister's body stiffen, and I realized she expected me to answer, to reassure her. I figured taking a different route might distract her best.

"What were you doing fucking him, then?"

"Oh I don't know, Davey." She sighed, laying back on the bed and putting her hands behind her head. "Why am I fucking you?"

"I guess they're both good questions."

"Well…" Her lips curved into a smile, sliding her hand over my thigh and settling over the bulge in my trousers. I couldn't be within a foot of her anymore without sporting wood. "Maybe if we don't ask the questions, we never need to learn the answers."

"I don't think it works that way."

"Maybe I should just keep my mouth busy, then." My stepsister slithered down onto the floor between my legs, looking up at me with that mischievous smile. I should have stopped her, but her hand rubbing the already stiffening length of my cock felt so good, and the promise of her mouth as she unzipped my trousers, those eager red lips and hungry pink tongue…

"Oh hell…" I watched through half-closed eyes as she took me into her mouth, half-hard but growing with every slow suck up and down my cock. I glanced toward the door and it occurred to me that Mum was right downstairs, that she could come up at any time, calling for either one of us. The thought made my heart leap and my stomach drop. "We can't! Dawn!"

She didn't stop, so I grabbed onto her hair, pulling her gently off. Her lips were even redder now, after just a few moments of sucking me. Her eyes were hungry, and she licked her lips, looking up at me, her smile downright wicked. "What's the matter, baby brother?"

"Mum could come in!" I hissed, glancing at the door again.

Dawn nodded, her hand moving up and down between my legs, my cock straining towards the warm wetness of her mouth. God, she could suck a cock! I wanted her. I wanted to shove that bikini top down and bury myself in the abundance of her breasts. I imagined the smooth, shaved swell of her pussy lips, sliding my cock head between them…

"Doesn't that make it even hotter?" she whispered, stroking my cock against her tits, tucking the head between her cleavage. "Knowing we could get caught… at any minute…"

She stood quickly, untying her bikini top and letting it fall, her breasts heavy and ripe and so luscious they made me actually begin to salivate. Then she pulled her bottoms down and turned around. I groaned softly when she reached back with both hands to spread herself wide, the round curve of her arse sloping down to reveal that hot, pink cleft, the place I dreamed about at night, so beautiful I thought if I looked there too long, I'd lose myself or die. She wiggled her arse back and forth slowly, looking at me from between her legs, her face framed by the pendulous sway of her breasts, her hair brushing the floor.

"Want some of that?" It was then – when she reached between her legs and grabbed hold of my cock – that I lost it. I forgot everything else – I forgot that Mum was downstairs arranging flowers and Dad was due home any minute and I was supposed to be going on a date with Jules in half an hour. I forgot everything but the captivating appeal of my stepsister's pussy, and even if I'd tried, even if I'd made the attempt to remember all of those things, there was no way to resist when she deftly positioned me against her hole and slid all the way down onto my cock like a fireman sliding down a pole.

"Oh Jesus!" I whispered, grabbing her arse and pulling the weight of her into the saddle of my hips. She leaned back, her hair spilling over my shoulder as she steadied herself with her palms on my thighs. My hands went naturally around, cupping her heavy breasts, their nipples hard and growing harder as I rolled them between thumb and finger. The feel of my cock so deep inside of her was bliss, so good I thought I would pass out – and then she began to move.

It wasn't a proper fuck – there was no thrusting involved. She moved her hips in splendid circles, grinding her arse down against me, making my cock writhe inside the encompassing heat of her flesh. She took my hand, moving it between her legs, helping me find her clit.

"Rub it, Davey," she murmured, dancing around on my prick. "Faster, baby, faster! Yes... yes! That's good!" I found the rhythm she liked, trying to keep up with her, our breath coming in short, harsh pants as we rocked together on the edge of the bed. Gasping, she slowed, digging her nails into my thighs, her hips still rocking slightly, more with the motion of my hand than anything else.

"Oh god... oh god... baby... sweet baby, yes, yes, make me come!" Her voice was barely above a whisper, urging me on, and my cock swelled inside of her at the thought of her impending orgasm. I worked at it, my fingers sliding through the wet heat of her flesh, moving across the hood of her sensitive, hidden clit, feeling her shiver in my lap. "Ummm... Ummmm... Ummmmmm..." The sound of her drove me starkers and I reached up with my other hand to grab her breast, squeezing and rolling her nipple, feeling her tense and stiffen.

"Oh!" Her orgasm surprised her, and the feel of her pussy spasming around my cock nearly ambushed me into climax, too. It was a delicious pull, the lure of the siren, the steady, rhythmic contractions of her flesh as she shuddered and rocked, losing her breath and finding it again a moment later in sharp gasps. She whimpered and sighed, sliding off my prick, leaving me wet and throbbing and aching for the heat of her cunt. Collapsing onto her belly on the bed, she looked over at me, now all content and satisfied.

"You are so fucking good." Her praise made both my ego and cock swell in unison. She reached between my legs, wrapping a lazy hand around me and thumbing the tip, back and forth, making me moan.

"Dawnie, please..."

She gave me a saucy smile, stroking me a little faster. "What's the matter, baby brother?"

I groaned, trying not to think anymore about the possibility of getting caught. I was peripherally aware, my ears tuned to the sound of someone on the stairs, the squeaky board on the landing, but the feel of my stepsister's hand tugging at my cock was too delicious to ignore. I wanted her – I wanted to fuck her senseless, make her scream. I wanted to come inside her so hard I saw stars and my ears rang.

"You started this." I got up, grabbing her hips and pulling her to her knees on the bed. She gave a short, surprised squeal but her body didn't protest. Her arse rose into the air, her pussy still swollen from her delectable dance on my cock. I slid my fingers through the wetness for a moment, taking myself in hand and pressing the head to the wet, peeking hole I ached to fill.

"Come on, Davey." She was teasing, squeezing the muscles of her pussy against the head of my dick. "Take that pussy. You know you want it."

That was a fucking understatement.

"You want to fuck your sister's cunt, don't you?" she murmured, the devilish tone in her voice taking me 'round the twist.

"Yes!" I hissed, grabbing her arse and driving myself deep. She moaned and arched back, meeting my thrust. "Fuck yes!"

I wanted it. I wanted it, and more importantly, I was taking it. She was mine, completely and utterly. No more Ken the wanker, nothing between us, we were flesh against flesh, buried again and again, like an exquisite secret I never wanted to be revealed. I took her because she was mine, she had always been mine, and as much as I wanted to deny it, to pretend it wasn't true – maybe I was afraid because I knew it really was so – fucking her was the closest I was ever going to come to complete. I never wanted it to end.

But Dawn was making those little squeaky noises again, her tell-tale "uh, uh, uh," and I was so close, I was getting loopy – the world was fading in and out with every thrust. When she came again, her fingers working between her legs, her tits swaying beneath her against the bed, she let out several long, low moans, each one successively louder – way too loud to be mistaken for anything other than they were. I heard something – I thought for sure I heard something, that squeaky step on the landing, maybe? Panicked, I looked toward the door, worried Mum had heard and was coming to investigate. I pumped faster into my stepsister's cunt, watching my cock disappear between the hot pink flesh, determined to come, come, come, I told myself I didn't care who might interrupt us at any minute…

"No!" Dawn shifted her hips forward, and although I grabbed for her, she was too fast and out of my reach. "I want it!" she insisted, turning and grabbing my aching cock. "I want your cum. Make me swallow it all, baby brother."

Fuck. That was it. I grabbed her by the hair, growling and thrusting my cock to the very back of her throat, not caring if she gagged – and she did, but she didn't seem to mind.

"Ahhhhh fuck!" I groaned. "Swallow it! Swallow it all, Dawnie!"

She grabbed the clench of my arse in her hands and pulled me in deeper, the sounds she made in her throat urging me on, and I exploded, convulsing uncontrollably and shooting hot jets of cum into her eager, waiting mouth. I heard her swallowing, and I gave her more, more, blasting her with so much of the stuff I wondered, for a brief, dizzy moment, if a man could hemorrhage from loss of semen.

She grinned at me, wiping her chin, her eyes bright. "Mmmm… more?"

"You're bad," I whispered, stroking her hair, feeling my cock waning wetly against my thigh.

"You like me that way."

She was right.

"Oh fuck!" I grabbed for my underwear and trousers, yanking them on. "I'm late."

"What for?" Dawn pulled a cover over her, looking disheveled and distracting with one thigh peeking out from under the sheet.

I sighed. "My date."

"Oh right." She rolled her eyes. "Jules the twat face?"

I reached for the doorknob, not wanting to look back at her. "Button it!"

"Don't you want to stay here with me?" Dawn pulled the sheet aside a little – I did look back, I couldn't help it – and I caught a glimpse of the sweetness I'd been buried in moments ago. "Mum and Dad are supposed to go out later."

I actually considered it. I stood there and weighed the appeal of my own stepsister as opposed to Julie. Then I shook my head, grimacing, and told her, "Dawn, no. I have to go."

I turned away from her pouty look, tried to block it out as I shut her door and headed down the hall. I went into the washroom, did a quick shave, brushed my hair and washed my teeth. I didn't notice Mum on the landing until I started down the stairs. I nearly jumped out of my skin at the sight of her sitting there—just… sitting there.

"Mum?"

She looked up at me, and I knew. *She knew.* Fuck. Her eyes were blank. "Going out, Davey?"

I nodded, swallowing past a lump in my throat. "You all right, Mum?"

"Fine." Her voice was distant. "Your dad will be home soon."

"I'll be late," I said, stepping past her on the stairs. "Real late."

"That's fine."

I wanted to escape. The thought that Mum knew – what had she heard? Anything? Did she really know? Why else would she be sitting on the landing, practically catatonic? I glanced back when I hit the bottom of the stairs. She was looking my way, but it was like she was looking past me.

What could I do? Undecided, I stood there another moment longer, looking at the front door, then back at Mum. Then it occurred to me – she was right. Dad would be home soon. If she *had* heard something… suspected something… and she told Dad when he came home? I didn't want to be anywhere near the house when that happened!

I put on my shoes, grabbed my jacket, and headed out the door.

Chapter Ten

I was supposed to meet Julie at the club, and she was standing outside waiting for me when I got there – decidedly late.

She didn't see me at first and I looked at her, leaning against the side of the building, her head turned the other way. Her dark hair fell in long, loose curls around the curve of her face in profile, and it naturally led my eyes downward to the curves of her body. She was slender and soft, the size of her breasts a delightful surprise, a continental shelf – the woman had two delicious, sizeable sweater muffins under there!

I was amazed she didn't seem annoyed I was late. She wasn't tapping her foot or pacing. She didn't even look bored – she was just there, in the moment. There was even a half smile on her face.

"Hey Jules!" I slipped my arm around her waist and she turned to me, that half-smile filling and brightening immediately. Even her eyes smiled.

"Hey sexy!" She turned her face up for a kiss expectantly, not doubting for a moment I would give her one – and I did, a long, soft kiss that deepened into something else as I pressed her against the wall, leaning my weight fully against her. She gasped when we parted, her eyes shining. "Wow! I wasn't expecting that."

"Let's not go in."

She raised her eyebrows. "Not go in?"

"I want to be with you." I nuzzled her neck, feeling her melt against me, the soft press of her breasts against my chest making me ache to touch them without any barrier between us. "Just you."

"Well... I was going to surprise you..." Her breath moved across my ear, making my cock twitch. "Joanna's gone to stay at Mum and Dad's for the weekend. She's standing up in a wedding."

I perked up – in more ways than one. "We have your whole flat to ourselves?"

"That's right." She waggled her eyebrows.

"What are we waiting for?" I kissed her again, harder this time, sliding my thigh between hers and wondering if she was wearing knickers – she still hardly ever did. I pushed her skirt up a little with my hand, feeling the impossibly soft skin of her thigh. She sighed and shifted against me, not protesting at all, even though people were all around us.

"Hey, ya randy bloke!" The sound of a voice behind me made me stop any further exploration. "Get a room!"

"We've got one!" I called back over my shoulder and then turned to Julie and whispered, "Let's go use it."

Julie shared a nice flat with her twin sister, Joanna, on Forest Road. I didn't fathom how they could make enough between them to afford it, but I think their Mum and Dad helped them out with groceries and such. We walked from the Tube, Julie swinging my hand and banging on about her late hours, and how hard her employer was working her lately. I paid only peripheral attention, the question of what was going on at home knotted like a viper in my belly.

"David, are you listening?"

"Huh?" I glanced at her as she unlocked the door to her flat and let us both in. The place smelled like roses and cats, a strange combination. They had a cat, even though they weren't supposed to have any pets.

"What can I do to get your mind back here?" Julie pondered, shutting the door and tossing her purse and keys on the foyer table. Her tone was teasing as she shrugged off her jacket and let it drop to the floor. She was dressed to the nines, ready for a night of dancing, and the sight of her breasts pushed up in some silky material transfixed me for a moment.

"That helped," I said, leaving off my shoes and stepping over her discarded jacket.

"What did?" She slid up onto the arm of a big, cushy chair, unbuckling the little straps on her heels and letting them clatter to the floor. "Oh, you mean this?" Her fingers worked the buttons on her blouse, pulling it free of her skirt to get the lower ones. Her blouse was sheer and black, her bra the clear decoration beneath. She stood and let her shirt drop to the floor, too, and went to work on her bra. "Is this helping get your mind back on... things?"

"More than my mind..."

The bra joined the growing pile of clothing on the floor and I stared as her breasts bounced free, their small, dark nipples already hard.

"Unzip me?" Julie turned, bending over the arm of the chair. Their cat – he was named something – Seymour? Simon? I couldn't remember – jumped up into the chair and mewed at her. She pet him, cooing and making soft noises that made my cock jump. I moved closer, running my hand along the smooth curve of her back as I slowly worked the zipper of her skirt down. She had a terrific set of arse antlers on her lower back, a tattoo like black lightning that met in the middle to form a heart-shape. I hadn't noticed it the first time we were together in my bedroom in the dark, but we'd managed to find other times this week to fuck like bunnies, squeezing it in between her work schedule and her flatmate's. I'd only seen Joanna a few times – a startling shock, since they were identical twins. But Joanna didn't have that hot tattoo on her back where Jules did.

If she was wearing knickers – and you never knew with Julie – I thought they would be black. Instead, they were white cotton with a little lace edge, quite prim. They made me smile. It was somehow even more alluring, those little girl-like panties underneath all the sexy outerwear. I slid her skirt down her slim hips, watching it pool at her feet.

"Nice knickers." I pulled them down to reveal all of her tattoo. Damn, that was hot.

"You like 'em?" Julie hooked her thumbs in and pulled them all the way off, turning and letting them dangle from her finger. "You can have 'em!"

I laughed as she tucked them into my jacket pocket, pressing herself against me. She was completely naked and my cock was rock hard as I grabbed onto her arse and pulled her close.

"Well, you've succeeded." I took her hand and placed it over my crotch, letting her feel how hard her little striptease had made me.

"I said I wanted your *mind* back." Julie giggled, squeezing the length of my cock through my trousers and making me jump. "Oh wait! I guess I *did* succeed, didn't I?"

I snorted. "All men think with their dicks, is that it?"

"What are you thinking now?" She sank slowly to her knees in front of me, letting every inch of her naked body rake down my fully clothed front, and I watched her feeling dizzy with lust. She unzipped me quickly and I was in her hand before I could even take another breath.

"Thinking?"

She giggled again and then ran the tip of her tongue around the head of my aching cock, making me groan. We'd squared away the sucks-like-a-Hoover issue on our second "date" – and she had made great progress in the blowjob department since. I loved the way she looked up at me when she did it, stopping now and then to ask, "Like this?" or "Good?"

All I could manage to respond was, "Fantastic! Fucking fantastic!" closing my eyes and letting the pleasure take me completely out of myself. She was actually making my knees weak!

"Jules," I gasped, pulling my cock out of her grasp. "I need to sit down or I'm going to collapse!"

She laughed and pushed me back toward the chair. I shrugged off my jacket and stepped out of my trousers on the way, while she followed me on her knees. Her mouth seemed to follow my cock and she latched on the moment I sat down, working up and down with a fervor that was going to make me blow way too soon for my liking.

"Wait." I reached for her, pulling her up so I could kiss her. I could taste myself in her mouth as she splayed herself between my legs. I couldn't help grabbing her arse and grinding my cock against her belly as we kissed. Julie wriggled and moaned when I spread her open with my hands.

"You didn't like my mouth?" she whispered, sucking on my neck – damn, she had a hard suck! I was going to have love bites in the morning. If she could only learn to use her powers for good!

"I love your mouth." I kissed her again, sucking at her lips, running my tongue along the sweet open flesh of her mouth. "But my cock is in the mood for some... brain food."

She giggled at my attempt at a joke, my fingers eagerly probing, her pussy hair soft and curly, giving way to the wetness beneath. There was nothing I wanted more in that moment than to be buried inside her.

"Come on, luv," I urged, helping her up so she was fully in my lap, straddling me. "Give my poor cock some nourishment."

"Only if you promise to give my little clitty some, too." She smiled again as she positioned herself, her hair a dark curtain around us as she grabbed hold and aimed me. I was falling in love with that smile.

"You couldn't keep my hands off it if you tried," I murmured as she sank down onto the length of my cock – fuck, that was good! Her breasts swayed slightly as she began to rock, balancing herself on the arms of the chair – they were ripe and luscious and I wanted to cup them but I restrained myself, using one hand on her hip to steady her and the other to find and focus on her clit.

"Ohhh yes." Her eyes closed, her hips pushing forward, making my cock shift to a delicious angle inside of her. "Rub it faster, Davey... faster..."

Hearing her call me Davey made me instantly think of my stepsister, and I didn't want to go there. I tried closing my eyes against it, but that brought her nearer – I could see Dawn's eyes glinting, the turn of her mouth and that mischievous smile. *I'm not fucking my sister.* I said it over and over in my head. *Not Dawn. Julie. Julie. Julie.*

"Julie!" I grabbed her hips, surprising her, I think. She was catching a good rhythm and losing herself and I had stopped that. "I... my..." What the hell was I going to say? Stop, because I keep thinking you're my sister? Christ! "I'm getting a cramp... can we...?"

"Oh!' She moved off me quickly, still startled, looking like she didn't know where to go, what to do, whether she should kneel or stand. She crossed her arms over her chest, biting her lip, and looked at me. I realized I was supposed to have a cramp and started rubbing my thigh.

"How about the bedroom?" I suggested, standing too, and pulling her against me, She looked so awkward and alone, and I wanted one of us, at least, to feel at ease. "Soft bed... soft music... soft skin..."

She grinned, reaching down to grasp my length. "As long as I get a hard cock."

"One hundred percent guaranteed."

"I'll meet you in my room." She kissed me softly on the cheek. "I have to use the loo."

Her room was twice the size of mine with a bed big enough for three. I turned on a lamp sitting on the nightstand, tossed my shirt aside and flopped on. I heard the sound of water running in the washroom next door and wondered what she was thinking. I wondered if she was thinking about what I was thinking. Hell, *I* didn't even want to be thinking what I was thinking.

I put my hands behind my head and closed my eyes, willing Julie to come back, because I was afraid to be with my own thoughts. I kept seeing the disappointment on Dawn's face when I left, the strangely catatonic look in Mum's eyes as I passed by. The guilt filling my chest threatened to choke me and I wanted to throw open a window and yell until my lungs felt free of it. I felt some sort of huge pressure, something weighing me down. It felt like everyone wanted a piece of me, wanted me to be something or do something for them. My head hurt. It felt like it was going to explode.

"Hey, luv." Julie sat on the edge of the bed on the other side. She had put on a t-shirt, a long one with Betty Boop on the front. "Do you want to talk about it?"

I stared at her, feeling a lump growing in my throat. "About how I keep all my brains in my dick, you mean?"

"I suppose." She smiled when she turned to look at me, but it wasn't the Julie smile I'd come to recognize. It was sadder, and full of a deeper understanding than I'd experienced with anyone I'd ever known. "She told me, David."

My heart stopped. Literally fucking stopped. "Who... what?"

"Dawn." Julie sighed, crawling up next to me and resting her head on the pillow beside mine. "Your sister?"

I didn't want to know. I asked anyway. "She told you... what?"

"She told me she was fucking you."

"Oh Christ." I covered my eyes with my arm, my stomach lurching. This couldn't be happening. What in the hell was Dawn thinking?

"And she told me to leave you alone."

"Oh... god..." I remembered my jealousy about Ken, how I'd fantasized about killing him. Had my stepsister really felt the same? "You must think..."

She touched my arm. "I'm here, aren't I?"

She was. The woman knew the worst possible thing I'd ever done (*it isn't, it isn't, you love her, you know you do, admit it, you love your sister and it isn't just a sisterly sort of love*) and still she was here. The next question that came to me made me sad: *Why?*

So now I was judging Julie for not judging me? What was wrong with me?

"I'm sorry." I wasn't sure who I was apologizing to – her, me or... everyone.

"Do you want to talk about it?" she asked again.

"I don't know."

"Why don't we just lie here, then?" She reached over me and turned out the light, snuggling up to my side. Her breath smelled like toothpaste, and I realized she'd brushed her teeth.

"All right."

"Things might look different in the morning."

Morning? That was my last thought before I drifted off.

* * * *

It wasn't quite dawn yet when I woke from terribly conflicted dreams filled with painfully archetypal unseen monsters and long quests. I knew immediately I wasn't home in my bed, but for a moment I forgot everything entirely, the disorienting feeling of being nothing, lost, not knowing where or even who I was, completely overwhelming. Then I felt her shift beside me, her breath against my shoulder, her arm folded in behind me like a soft wing, and I remembered – *Julie.*

"Morning, sexy." Her arm unfolded and she slid a hand down my belly.

I swallowed, afraid of my own voice. "How can you even look at me?"

"How could I not?" Her hand snuck slowly south, petting my skin, making me shiver. "You're a mighty fine sight in my bed in the morning,"

I blinked, stunned. "You're quite something."

"Thank you." Her hand moved lower, finding me at a quarter-mast – I was always at least a little hard in the morning. "Now, I think I remember someone promising me a hard cock and a little attention on a certain part of my anatomy…"

"That's right, isn't it?" I turned and kissed her, trying to put every grateful feeling I had into that kiss. She arched and sighed and pressed her naked thigh between mine, like the slide of satin, her breasts full against my chest.

"I dreamed about fucking you," she whispered, her hands in my hair, leading me – as if I needed leading – to the rising mounds of her breasts. Her nipples were hard already and I licked and sucked them, listening to her moan as she told me about her dream. "I was bent over the kitchen table, and you were spanking me, telling me what a bad girl I was." The thought made my cock spring to full attention, and I traced faster circles with my tongue around her nipple. "And every time you spanked my bottom, I felt it in my pussy."

I groaned, slipping my hand down to her mound, rocking it over the fullness of her pussy. She moaned, too, getting a little more breathless, but she didn't stop telling me.

"You kept saying I needed to be punished," she murmured, pressing with her hips against my hand, begging with her body for more. "And then you spread my legs and put your cock inside me."

That thought had my cock throbbing and I reached a hand down to quell the ache a little. She didn't stop: "You fucked me hard, right from the first." Julie sighed and opened wider when my fingers found their way through her wet, pink flesh, parting the dark, curly hair and probing. "And every time you... oh!" My fingers slid in deep and she shuddered, clutching me. "Every time you shoved into me, you said 'Bad!'... mmmmm... like that..." She moved her hips in circles, her pussy squeezing my fingers. "Just like that... you kept saying, 'bad, bad, bad'..."

"I'm the bad one," I confessed, feeling somehow connected to her dream. Had I been punishing her somehow for what I had done with my stepsister? "Julie, I wish she hadn't told you..."

"I'm glad she told me," she insisted, putting her hand over mine between her thighs. "I don't want to have any secrets between us."

"Christ!" I shook my head, blinking at her. "This isn't a secret, it's a... an abomination!"

"Things happen. It was a natural mistake." She rocked, rocked, her eyes half-closed. "You were lonely... and, I imagine, really fucking randy."

"You don't find me disgusting?"

"Rather not..." She smiled. "I just want to know one thing." I knew what the question was and I didn't want to answer it. I was afraid of my response. "Do you want to keep on with her?"

Fuck. Did I? My head was filled with Dawn's mischievous smile, her full hips, her nasty talk and hot fucking ways...

"No." I lied. I lied and tried to make myself believe the lie. "I don't want her." The truth was a little deeper than that. *I can't have her.* "Especially with you in my bed."

"*My* bed," she reminded me. "But I don't see why it can't be yours, too..."

I understood immediately what she was proposing. "What about your sister?"

"My sister's easy... in every sense of the word." Julie smiled, leaning in to whisper into my ear. "And she bats for both sides..."

It took me a moment to understand the full meaning of what she was saying. Joanna liked fillies as well as blokes? And just how did Julie know... my eyes widened and I stared. Had she and her sister... *her own sister*...? I was gob smacked. The question must have been in my eyes.

"Yes," Julie nodded, her eyes bright, her hand still rocking over mine, driving my fingers into her wetness, and I knew she was answering my unasked question, not just exclaiming over the sensation between her legs. Feeling stunned, my cock harder than it had ever been in my life, I slid between her thighs to reward her for her understanding, her acceptance. I licked her pussy like I was begging for absolution, seeking redemption, and in part, I was.

"Oh yes, yes!" she murmured, reaching down to spread her lips wide so I could delve deep with my tongue, my nose rubbing against the nub of her clit. Her taste was darker, stronger – god, I didn't want to keep comparing them. I shoved the thought out of my head, just focusing on her clit, watching her belly undulate as her hips rolled, her hands cupping her own breasts, pulling at her nipples. My cock pressed hard against the bedclothes and I fucked them slowly, watching her and imagining my cock sliding into the wetness my fingers were probing.

"Oh fuck, fuck, that's it! That's so fucking IT!" Her hips shot up against my mouth and I had to grab her with both hands, lashing my tongue over her pussy with great fervor, working hard for her come, wanting it, and she gave it to me in hot, rolling waves, her whole body shuddering with pleasure. She came down slowly, whispering, "oh... oh... ohhh," her head going back and forth on the pillow. I was dizzy with lust now, blind with it, and I sucked my fingers drenched in her juices.

"I want to fuck you," I told her, grabbing her hips and rolling her quickly to her belly. I wanted to see that tattoo, watch it while she fucked back against my aching cock. She gasped but acquiesced, lifting her arse in the air, using two fingers from underneath to spread her lips, showing me the way – but my cock already knew. I let him lead, closing my eyes and just driving forward, finding that sweet, wet hole and thrusting deep.

"Oh god!" She moaned, and I felt her fingers staying there, rubbing at her little clit. I knew I wasn't going to last long, and I grasped her hips for leverage, my thumbs rubbing over that black lightning tattoo, massaging and spreading it as I began to fuck her. She was hot inside, very tight and oh-so-sweet, like driving into wet silk, and I rolled my hips, trying to hold out a little. The head of my cock felt the size of a football shoved inside her, rubbing into the soft niches of her flesh.

"Ahhhh yes," I groaned, feeling her pussy squeeze my length. "You feel so fucking good!"

"You like that?" She rolled her hips in circles to match mine, squeezing her pussy and releasing, driving me batty. "Feel good all over that hard cock?"

"Fuck!" I tried to hold it, I tried, but her pussy clenched and clenched, milking me.

"I love you fucking me," she moaned, slapping back against me, my balls brushing her hand where she was furiously rubbing her clit. "That's it! Harder! Fuck that pussy hard, baby!"

Oh, bloody fucking hell. There was no holding out. I couldn't possibly.

"Julie!" I cried out her name, reassuring myself, knowing it was Julie's body writhing against me, Julie's cunt squeezing me and on the verge of coming again, too. "Oh fuck, Julie, you're going to make me come!"

She moaned, reaching back to feel my cock plunging into her. "Come all over my arse!" she begged me. "I want to feel it!"

Oh damn. I was right there! I jerked myself quickly out of the wet warmth of her cunt, and the first blast hit the fingers she was using to bring herself off. She gasped in surprise, then moaned and began to shudder, her arse rolling with her orgasm. I knew she was coming, too, because she told me.

"Oh yesss! Coming! Coming!" She shook with it. I watched her body roll and grabbed my spurting cock, aiming it last-minute at her arse, shooting thick, white spurts over the hot splash of her tattoo, watching it drip down in clearish white streams, my cock jerking, my balls so tight, drawn up to empty their load completely, every spasm bringing a wicked shudder of pleasure.

The first thing I wanted to ask, once I could breathe and speak normally again, was if Julie had really been trying to tell me that she'd been with her own sister. But I couldn't get up the nerve. Instead, we took a long, hot shower, soaping each other up. It was sexy and sweet, but I was too hungry and too worried about what might be going on at home to think about having another go.

"What do you want for brekkie?" Julie stood on one foot in front of the open refrigerator when I came in wearing just my trousers and drying my hair with a towel.

"Food," I replied, sitting at the table. "Hungry!'

"How about a fry-up?" Julie starting pulling things out of the refrigerator. "Eggs and sausages?"

"Sounds fantastic." I glanced over at the phone, knowing I should call, but not wanting to. It was ten in the morning and Mum was going to be furious. I was surprised she hadn't rung already, off her head. "Can I use your phone?"

Julie glanced over, smiling. "Got to call your Mum?"

"If I don't, I'm gonna be completely jaspered." I didn't tell her I was worried maybe Mum had seen or heard something she shouldn't have. As comfortable as Julie seemed about knowing I'd slept with my stepsister, I still just wasn't all that used to the idea yet.

"Mum?"

"David? Oh good," she said. I blinked at the phone. She didn't sound mad at all. "Are you at Julie's then?"

"Yeah."

"Good." Good again? What in the bloody hell was going on? "Just be home at a decent time tonight."

"Yeah," I repeated, knowing my voice sounded strange, rather strangled, but I couldn't help it. I'd already stayed out all night long, and not only was she not pitching a fit, she wasn't insisting I come home immediately to accept my punishment! Who was this woman, and what had she done with my Mum?

"Bye, then!" With that, Mum hung up.

That was it? I stared at Julie, bewildered. The thing in my belly that had been there since Dawn and I had started up was churning.

"How did it go?" Julie was frying up eggs.

"Mum wasn't upset." I stared at the phone in my hand, still incredulous. "Said I should just get home at a decent hour tonight."

"That's rare then?" She reached for the salt and pepper, and I couldn't help notice how her t-shirt rode up, showing me the curve of her bottom.

"Rare as rocking horse shit," I agreed. There was something wrong with this picture, I just couldn't put my finger on it.

"Well, then, we have all day." She winked at me, stirring the sausages in another pan. "Joanna won't be back until late tonight."

I put the phone on the table and went over to her. "Maybe we should kick her out for the whole week," I said, kissing her neck. She turned her head to let me, and I swear if she was a cat, she would have purred. "Just stay in bed."

She laughed. I loved that laugh. "You're going to get me sacked! Just because you don't have a job..."

"I'm going to have to find one." I sighed, burying my face in and breathing the scent of her clean hair. "Dad's threatening to cut off my pocket money starting next week."

"You'll find one." She flipped the eggs. "You're resourceful."

"That's true." I peered over her shoulder, sliding my hands around to cup her breasts and thumb her nipples. "I'm also hungry. Let's eat!"

"Mmmm!" She shivered, pressing her bottom back against me. "Hold your horses, sexy. Everything in due time."

Everything.

That's what I wanted.

Everything.

And that's just what I couldn't have.

* * * *

"Mum?"

She was sitting on the sofa when I came in, flipping through the telly. I could count on one hand the times I'd seen my Mum just sitting in front of the telly.

"Oh, there you are." She smiled at me, but she seemed distracted. "Did you have fun at Julie's?"

Fun? What I'd had at Julie's couldn't be called anything but, I suppose, but she said it like I was five and coming home from a play date at a friend's house. She had to have known what we were doing.

"Uh… yeah." It was a Sunday evening, and I expected Dad to be the one on the sofa snoozing in front of the telly, Dawn to be up in her room playing music loud enough for Mum to tell her to turn it down while she read a book in the chair next to Dad… "Where is everyone?"

Mum shrugged. "Out."

I decided not to press my luck and went upstairs, glancing at Dawn's room at the end of the hall just out of habit as I opened my bedroom door. What I saw made me stop and stare.

Her door was open, but there was nothing in it. *Nothing* – her bed, her desk, her computer, her stereo, even the posters of Sting on the wall. It was all gone. I had to check for myself I wasn't hallucinating, going past Mum and Dad's closed bedroom door, and pushing my stepsister's fully open.

The carpet was pink – it had been since she was twelve and Mum had gone through a redecorating phase – the walls covered with a shiny white wallpaper, like striped satin. Her curtains were still the pink roses she'd picked out when she was twelve – mine were blue stars and moons because I'd been going through an outer space thing at the time. It looked like a little girl's room completely, now that her stuff was out of it.

And just what was her stuff doing out of it?

I bounded down the stairs, and Mum turned her face to me as I stopped in front of her. "Mum? Where's all Dawn's stuff?"

She didn't even blink. "Oh, she's moved into Laurie's flat."

My heart sunk and I just knew... Mum *had* heard. Had heard, and had acted, quickly and cleanly, kicking Dawn out of the house. No wonder she hadn't cared how long I stayed at Jules'!

"Is she there now?"

Mum shook her head, going back to the telly. "She's at the health club, giving her notice."

"Her..." *Notice? She's quitting her job?*

Mum ignored my confusion. "Laurie's got her in. They needed another shop assistant."

"I'm going out." I couldn't think. I needed to see my stepsister, talk to her...

"Again?"

"I'll be back in an hour."

At least, I thought I would.

* * * *

She was coming out as I was going in. We stood there for a moment, just looking at each other, the weight of what we'd done, how we felt, what we knew, hovering over us like an anvil. And then it fell. She threw her arms around me and I held her, right there in front of the health club with people walking in and out around us.

"I'm so sorry, David," she whispered against my neck, and I felt the hot wetness of her tears.

"We need to go somewhere." I meant away from the entrance of the health club – at least, that's what I meant out loud. What I really meant was we had to go away together, run away somewhere, live happily ever after.

"Come on." She took my hand and led me around the side of the building. Parking was in back, so it was quiet here, and she squeezed my hand as she stopped. "Mum knows."

I nodded. "I know."

"Did she say anything to you?"

"No." I shook my head. "What did she say to you?"

"She told me she and Dad had talked about it and decided I needed to find my own place."

I stared at her. "Did she say... she heard... or saw...?"

"Mum?" Dawn snorted. "She'd never. No... she just said she'd already talked to Laurie, who said I could move in with her. Dad rented a lorry and helped me move my stuff. It happened... very fast."

"Overnight!" I shook my head, shoving my hands into my pockets. "She told me to stay at..."

"Julie's." Dawn swallowed, looking at me. "David, I did an awful thing..."

"More awful than what we've been doing?"

"That hasn't been awful!" She slipped her arms around me, resting her head against my chest. "Do you think it's been awful?"

I didn't want to tell her how amazing, how beautiful, how incredible... "I know you told Jules."

"Oh, David, I'm so sorry."

I kissed the top of her blonde head. "She doesn't care."

"She's..." I felt her sobs. She was doing it silently, as if I wouldn't know. I wanted to make it all okay, and I just couldn't. She gave a hitching breath and said, "She'll be good for you."

"I want..." I lifted her face in my hands, kissed the tears off her cheeks. Her eyes said everything, and I knew mine must, too. "Oh Dawnie, I want you. God help me. I do."

"I know." Tears just continued to fall from her eyes like rain. "But you know we can't."

I didn't want to know it, but I did. I kissed her as if to chase it away, tasting the salt of her tears, licking it from her lips. I didn't want any evidence of pain left when we were through.

"David..."

I shook my head, pulling her to me again and holding her. "I'm going to leave home. Move in with Jules."

"That's probably best." She trembled in my arms as if it were cold outside instead of a warm summer evening. "Mum and Dad…"

"They won't ever talk about it again, Dawnie."

"No." The flat tone of her voice told me she knew it was true. We wouldn't ever have to say anything to them, to admit to our parents what we'd done. But they would always know. And so would we.

"Oh, I meant to tell you…" She moved away, wiping at her cheeks with her hands, trying to compose herself. "I gave my notice and talked you up quite a bit. My boss was very interested. The job's yours if you want it."

"Thank you." I didn't know what else to say.

She smiled, a brave-girl sort of smile, the kind she always gave me whenever Mum and Dad were fighting when we were little and she was trying to cheer me up and let me know it was all going to be okay. "I'm going to miss you."

"I'm not going anywhere." I reached out to clasp her hand, wanting more of her and afraid to ask for it. "I'm your brother."

"You know what I mean." She squeezed back.

"Yeah. Yeah I do."

She pulled away, slinging her purse over her shoulder. "I'm going to go home."

I was going to say let's go together, and then I realized, we didn't live in the same home together anymore. "All right."

"I love you, David." Her eyes were shining, and they said it all. The words meant nothing, everything, and I fought the urge to reach for her again, to give into what I knew was wrong and wanted anyway.

"I love you, too."

I think she heard me as she was 'rounding the corner. I hope she did.

* * * *

Mum and Dad were at work, and all my stuff was already over at Julie's. My room was completely empty, with its sky blue carpet and glowing stars on the ceiling, looking as stuck-in-time as Dawn's had when she'd left.

There was just one thing left to do. I took a large rubbish bag and headed out to the shed. They were all still there, the dirty mags I'd hidden so Mum and Dad wouldn't find them. I'd been so afraid of being discovered. And now...

I grabbed a handful of magazines and shoved them into the bag, my eyes stinging, my vision blurred. The pages were slippery, and one of the magazines slid out of my hands, spilling onto the floor. *Naughty Bits*. I picked it up, flipping through, remembering how many times I'd come out to this shed to look at these pictures, imagining what it might be like to be with a woman like this.

There... there was the page. Dawn's writing in the margin, fat and curly with a heart over the "i": *"She looks like me."*

She really did.

I tore the page out, folding it carefully, and put it into my back pocket. Then I finished bagging the rest, swiping at my eyes before tossing the heavy bag into the bin with the rest of the rubbish.

The End

ABOUT SELENA KITT

Like any feline, Selena Kitt loves the things that make her purr-and wants nothing more than to make others purr right along with her! Pleasure is her middle name, whether it's a short cat nap stretched out in the sun or a long kitty bath. She makes it a priority to explore all the delightful distractions she can find, and follow her vivid and often racy imagination wherever it wants to lead her.

Her writing embodies everything from the spicy to the scandalous, but watch out-this kitty also has sharp claws and her stories often include intriguing edges and twists that take readers to new, thought-provoking depths.

When she's not pawing away at her keyboard, Selena runs an innovative publishing company (www.excessica.com) and in her spare time, she devotes herself to her family—a husband and four children—and her growing organic garden. She also loves bellydancing and photography.

Her books *EcoErotica* (2009), *The Real Mother Goose* (2010) and *Heidi and the Kaiser* (2011) were all Epic Award Finalists. Her only gay male romance, *Second Chance*, won the Epic Award in Erotica in 2011. Her story, *Connections*, was one of the runners-up for the 2006 Rauxa Prize, given annually to an erotic short story of "exceptional literary quality," out of over 1,000 nominees, where awards are judged by a select jury and all entries are read "blind" (without author's name available.)

She can be reached on her website at
www.selenakitt.com

BABYSITTING THE BAUMGARTNERS
By Selena Kitt

Ronnie—or as Mrs. Baumgartner insists on calling her, Veronica—has been babysitting for the Baumgartners since she was fifteen years old and has practically become another member of the family. Now a college freshman, Ronnie jumps at the chance to work on her tan in the Florida Keys with "Doc" and "Mrs. B" under the pretense of babysitting the kids. Ronnie isn't the only one with ulterior motives, though, and she discovers that the Baumgartners have wayward plans for their young babysitter. This wicked hot sun and sand coming of age story will seduce you as quickly as the Baumgartners seduce innocent Ronnie and leave everyone yearning for more!

Warning: This title contains MFF threesome, lesbian, and anal sex.

EXCERPT from
BABYSITTING THE BAUMGARTNERS:

When my legs felt steady enough to hold me, I got out of the shower and dried off, wrapping myself in one of the big white bath sheets. My room was across the hall from the bathroom, and the Baumgartner's was the next room over. The kids' rooms were at the other end of the hallway.

As I made my way across the hall, I heard Mrs. B's voice from behind their door. "You want that tight little nineteen-year-old pussy, Doc?"

I stopped, my heart leaping, my breath caught. *Oh my God.* Were they talking about me? He said something, but it was low, and I couldn't quite make it out. Then she said, "Just wait until I wax it for you. It'll be soft and smooth as a baby."

Shocked, I reached down between my legs, cupping my pussy as if to protect it, standing there transfixed, listening. I stepped closer to their door, seeing it wasn't completely closed, still trying to hear what they were saying. There wasn't any noise, now.

"Oh God!" I heard him groan. "Suck it harder."

My eyes wide, I felt the pulse returning between my thighs, a slow, steady heat. Was she sucking his cock? I remembered what it looked like in his hand--even from a distance, I could tell it was big--much bigger than any of the boys I'd ever been with.

"Ahhhh fuck, Carrie!" He moaned. I bit my lip, hearing Mrs. B's first name felt so wrong, somehow. "Take it all, baby!"

All?! My jaw dropped as I tried to imagine, pressing my hand over my throbbing mound. Mrs. B said something, but

I couldn't hear it, and as I leaned toward the door, I bumped it with the towel wrapped around my hair. My hand went to my mouth and I took an involuntary step back as the door edged open just a crack. I turned to go to my room, but I knew that they would hear the sound of my door.

"You want to fuck me, baby?" she purred. "God, I'm so wet ... did you see her sweet little tits?"

"Fuck, yeah," he murmured. "I wanted to come all over them."

Hearing his voice, I stepped back toward the door, peering through the crack. The bed was behind the door, at the opposite angle, but there was a large vanity table and mirror against the other wall, and I could see them reflected in it. Mrs. B was completely naked, kneeling over him. I saw her face, her breasts swinging as she took him into her mouth. His cock stood straight up in the air.

"She's got beautiful tits, doesn't she?" Mrs. B ran her tongue up and down the shaft.

"Yeah." His hand moved in her hair, pressing her down onto his cock. "I want to see her little pussy so bad. God, she's so beautiful."

"Do you want to see me eat it?" She moved up onto him, still stroking his cock. "Do you want to watch me lick that sweet, shaved cunt?"

I pressed a cool palm to my flushed cheek, but my other hand rubbed the towel between my legs as I watched. I'd never heard anyone say that word out loud and it both shocked and excited me.

"Oh God, yeah!" He grabbed her tits as they swayed over him. I saw her riding him, and knew he must be inside of her. "I want inside her tight little cunt."

I moved the towel aside and slipped my fingers between my lips.

He's talking about me!

The thought made my whole body tingle, and my pussy felt on fire. Already slick and wet from my orgasm in the shower, my fingers slid easily through my slit.

"I want to fuck her while she eats your pussy." He thrust up into her, his hands gripping her hips. Her breasts swayed as they rocked together. My eyes widened at the image he conjured, but Mrs. B moaned, moving faster on top of him.

"Yeah, baby!" She leaned over, her breasts dangling in his face. His hands went to them, his mouth sucking at her nipples, making her squeal and slam down against him even harder. "You want her on her hands and knees, her tight little ass in the air?"

He groaned, and I rubbed my clit even faster as he grabbed her and practically threw her off him onto the bed. She seemed to know what he wanted, because she got onto her hands and knees and he fucked her like that, from behind. The sound of them, flesh slapping against flesh, filled the room.

They were turned toward the mirror, but Mrs. B had her face buried in her arms, her ass lifted high in the air. Doc's eyes looked down between their legs, like he was watching himself slide in and out of her.

"Fuck!" Mrs. B's voice was muffled. "Oh fuck, Doc! Make me come!"

He grunted and drove into her harder. I watched her shudder and grab the covers in her fists. He didn't stop, though--his hands grabbed her hips and he worked himself into her over and over. I felt weak-kneed and full of heat, my fingers rubbing my aching clit in fast little circles. Mrs.

B's orgasm had almost sent me right over the edge. I was very, very close.

"That tight nineteen-year-old cunt!" He shoved into her. "I want to taste her." He slammed into her again. "Fuck her." And again. "Make her come." And again. "Make her scream until she can't take anymore."

I leaned my forehead against the doorjamb for support, trying to control how fast my breath was coming, how fast my climax was coming, but I couldn't. I whimpered, watching him fuck her and knowing he was imagining me ... *me!*

"Come here." He pulled out and Mrs. B turned around like she knew what he wanted. "Swallow it."

He knelt up on the bed as she pumped and sucked at his cock. I saw the first spurt land against her cheek, a thick white strand of cum, and then she covered the head with her mouth and swallowed, making soft mewing noises in her throat. I came then, too, shuddering and shivering against the doorframe, biting my lip to keep from crying out.

When I opened my eyes and came to my senses, Mrs. B was still on her hands and knees, focused between his legs-- but Doc was looking right at me, his dark eyes on mine.

He saw me. For the second time today--he saw me.

My hand flew to my mouth and I stumbled back, fumbling for the doorknob behind me I knew was there. I finally found it, slipping into my room and shutting the door behind me. I leaned against it, my heart pounding, my pussy dripping, and wondered what I was going to do now.

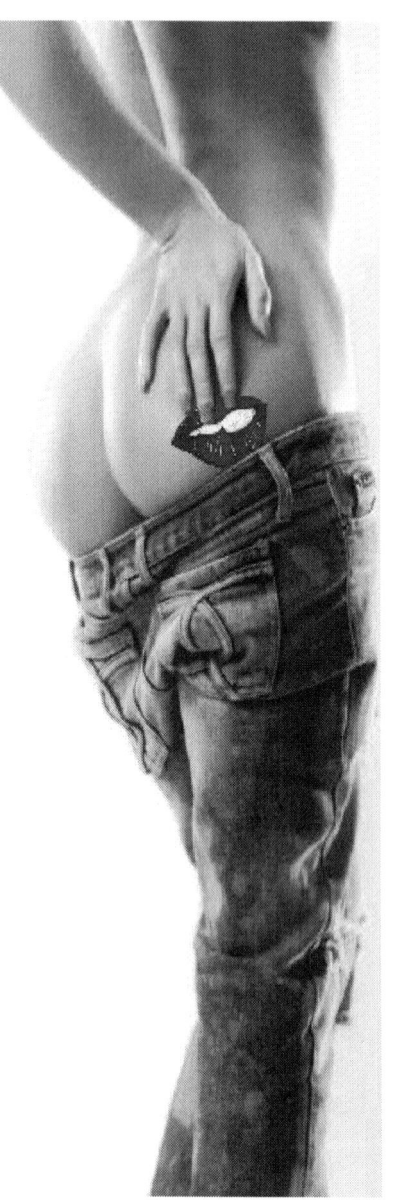

5696385R00091

Printed in Great Britain
by Amazon.co.uk, Ltd.,
Marston Gate.